A PIECE OF
THE WORLD

Mildred Walker

Illustrated by Christine Price

UNIVERSITY OF NEBRASKA PRESS
LINCOLN AND LONDON

First Bison Books printing: 2001

Library of Congress Cataloging-in-Publication Data
Walker, Mildred, 1905–
A piece of the world / Mildred Walker; illustrated by Christine Price.
p. cm.
Summary: While visiting her grandmother in Vermont, a young girl's
discovery of a huge boulder in the woods of a nearby farm leads her
into a special friendship with a boy living there.
ISBN 0-8032-9823-4 (pbk.: alk. paper)
[1. Friendship—Fiction.   2. Vermont—Fiction.]   I. Price, Christine,
1928– ill.   II. Title.
PZ7.W15363 Pi   2001
[Fic]—dc21
2001027710

*For my eight grands,
especially Matthew*

A PIECE OF
THE WORLD

1

"So, Calder, the best thing for you is to go to Gran's."

Calder stood by the window, her back toward her mother, looking down toward the pool that wouldn't be theirs after next week, nor the secret place back of the hibiscus bush. They would be sold; were sold already.

"I don't suppose you remember much about Weldon. You were only five when we were there; that would be seven years ago."

But Calder thought she did remember—sort of. Gran's house had a steep staircase. Outside everything was green, and the house was white. She thought she remembered a kind of park across from the house.

"You'll have a fine summer where I used to spend all my

3

summers when I was growing up. And when you come back, we'll be moved and your room will be all ready for you.''

Calder was busy separating the *we's*. The we in "when we were there" meant all of them, her and Dad and Mother; and the "we'll be moved" meant only Mother and her.

"See you, Calder," Dad had said, giving her their wink that meant more than kissing her and hugging her tight; it meant that everything was all right. But his leaving them wasn't all right. And she couldn't really believe even yet his going away to marry Lisa, even though she liked Lisa. Lisa was fun. Calder would like going to live with Dad and Lisa, but Mother said she couldn't bear that, and Dad said Mother needed her. Calder wished Mother needed her to help move, instead of saying she needed a space by herself for just a bit. "It's like when you want to go off to your hideout in the garden, Calder," Mother explained. And, of course, she did understand, only—

Calder turned around to look at Mother. With her hair all bubbly around her head and in her old yellow linen shorts and a shirt, she looked younger than any other mother Calder knew; lots younger than Lisa.

Calder said again, "I could help you move, though. I'd like to.''

"No, Calder, that's a miserable business, and I don't want you in on it. And I'll be terribly busy doing extra broadcasts while Ben is on vacation. By the time you come back, I'll be on my regular schedule again, so I won't be working so hard.''

That was partly the trouble: Mother's job on television. It

4

took up so much of her time, and it meant that she had to live on a schedule—and Dad hated schedules. She was always having to meet people and go out to luncheon and dinner with them, too. Mother had explained that it had been hard on Dad "I don't blame him, really," she had said. "But I have to be myself, too, and live my own life." Calder understood all that. Dad had explained it to her.

"And Gran is so happy that you're coming," Mother was saying. "It all works out splendidly. Think of flying all the way across the country alone!'' Mother swooped down on her and held her tight in her arms. And then Calder saw that there were tears in Mother's eyes, and she was ready to go to Timbuktu if Mother wanted her to.

That night Calder was almost asleep when she began to remember something: she was very little, and she was on Dad's back. They were going some place—woods, that was it, because she reached out and took hold of a branch, and Dad said the old horse would dump her if she did that again. She remembered as clear as anything! But she couldn't remember anything more. It must have been that time they went to Gran's; when they had all gone.

Dear Mother:
Here I am, all unpacked. I'm in your old room, but it doesn't seem much like you. Gran, who wants me to call her Mardie, the way you do, only I keep forgetting, says you always kept it (the room) very neat. Did you? I like the way you can see the hill from the bed, and the way the front window has a seat under it, and you can look out on the common.
Gran met me at the airport and was very jolly and talky. She has a new jeep. It was fun riding in it. She is disappointed to have me instead of you, I think, or at least, you and me together. She says you never say enough about yourself when you write. She asked lots of questions about you, and said you're a wonderful woman. (I think so, too.)
There don't seem to be many kids here my age. Gran had a girl who's spending the summer here with her grandparents come down for lunch yesterday. It was kind of sticky at first, but afterwards we played tennis and then

6

went swimming in a pool without any cement sides to it, just dug out of the ground. The water is very cold. The girl, whose name is Barbie Neale, is fat and hates it here, except that she's just met a boy she likes. He was out at the swimming pool, too. His name is Randy. Right away she asked me if I dated. Do you think Jerry coming over to use our pool, and playing tennis with him, could rate as a date? Anyway, I said I did, but it isn't really what she means.

Weldon is smaller than I ever imagined any village could be. Gran—I mean Mardie—says you spent all your summers here and just loved it. What did you do?

Mardie has a poodle named Vivacity! She calls her Viva. It sounds sorta silly, and Viva isn't all that lively. Are you all moved?

Bushels of love, Calder.

P.S. 1.   People get mixed up when they hear that my first name is the same as Gran's last one. Today the store-keeper said, "You're the Calder girl, aren't you? What's your first name?" When I said it was Calder, he said, "Calder-Calder," and laughed. I told him my last name was Bailey, but when I went out, he said "Good-by, Calder-Calder." He thinks he's very funny.
P.S. 2.   Gran found your old bicycle and had it fixed up for me. It's good to have to get around the town, but boy! is it old! One pedal has the rubber half worn off, and no gears, of course!

When Calder had sealed and stamped her letter, she rode up to the post office on her bicycle. If she got a good start, she could take the hill and arrive in front with a flourish. She dropped her letter in the slot inside the office and came out into the bright cool sun. It was funny not to be hot in summer. No wonder so few people here had any really good tan!

But then there wasn't anything to do but go back home—to Gran's. She stopped in the store and bought a lime popsicle, and the store-keeper called her Calder-Calder. Boys usually sat on the bench outside the store, but there weren't any there now, so she sat on the bench to eat her popsicle. Maybe some boy would come along. Barbie said there weren't any neat ones except Randy. But Dad always said she must make up her own mind about people and not go by what other people said about them.

She watched the bakery truck pull up, and then some people who must be from the Inn. You could tell right off by the slow way they walked along, but mostly by their clothes. Two men came in and out fast with cans of beer and were more fun to watch. They sat in the cab of their truck until they'd finished their beer. And then she was through with her popsicle and there wasn't any excuse for just sitting there, so she went on home. This was only the first week of June, and Mother wanted her to stay until the middle of August! Maybe if she wrote her after she was through moving, Mother would say she could go home sooner.

2

"I kinda remember being here with Dad and Mother," Calder said at lunch.

"Do you, dear? You were only five; I'm afraid you couldn't remember very much."

"I do, though. I remember how low the ceilings were, and Dad carrying me through the house on his shoulders, and somebody—Mother prob'ly—saying he'd hit my head, and I ducked it down behind his."

"Well, I'm sure he did that. He was always a boisterous sort of man, wanting Jean to go some place all the time. He must have dragged your mother up every hill around here. Other times, he'd spend the whole day lying in the hammock reading and not lift a finger to help with you.

9

Such an erratic person! I don't know how Jean put up with him so long."

Erratic was a queer word. Calder listened to it in her head, but she didn't ask what it meant because she didn't like Mardie talking about Dad. Anyway, you could almost tell what some words meant by the way people said them. Erratic was something not good, at least in Mardie's eyes, which didn't mean it was bad in hers! Something about always doing things other people didn't do. Like Dad making the motor of the car keep time to "Friday Night Has Come at Last, Sweedle-lee, bum-bum," when he picked her up at school on Fridays, and they sang it on the way home so loud that people on the street stared at them. And then she thought of Dad going off to the lake and staying two weeks because the book he was writing wouldn't go and never calling once, so Mother was wild. Writing a book made a father different from other fathers; it would be better maybe if he did something else—something with regular hours—but she couldn't imagine Dad doing something else. And it was nice having him at home so much. She could always tell by his tone of voice whether he was still thinking about his book or about her when he said, "Hello, Calder Cassiopeia Bailey," or "Calder Calliope Bailey," or "Calder Carnivora Bailey," and if he really wasn't thinking about her at all, she knew enough to say hello and go on without bothering him. He could even go out with her to the kitchen to get something to eat, still thinking about his book. Mother told him he gained weight when he was writing because he kept eating between meals, and Dad didn't like it. Calder had never read one of his books. She wondered if Mardie had them.

" . . . and completely undependable!" Mardie was still talking about Dad, straightening her knife and spoon with a quick cross movement of her hand. "He never appreciated your mother. My, you must have been thrilled to watch her on television every noon!"

"I didn't usually see her. She came on when I was at school." It made her uncomfortable to see Mother on TV; to hear her, especially. She sounded like Mother and like somebody else, at the same time.

"Come here, darling, and give Mardie a kiss," Gran said suddenly.

Calder went reluctantly. It was so funny Mardie's wanting to kiss her in the middle of a meal, and when she'd just been so cross about Dad. Calder wasn't particularly fond of being kissed or held tight like that.

"I'm going over to see Barbie," Calder said, wanting to get away. She might get Barbie to go up that hill that came down into town at the end of the main street.

"That's a fine idea," Gran said. "I'm going to be busy arranging a new display in the window of the shop. When you come back, you must tell me how you like it. Some time, I'm going to get you to help me in the shop, Calder. Would you enjoy that?"

"I guess so," Calder said, but she wasn't sure. It was an antique shop in the barn, and it was so full of glass stuff you had to watch all the time so you didn't knock anything down. She hadn't really looked at it hard. "Can Viva come with me?"

11

Mardie laughed. "She could if you could persuade her, but she never goes away if I'm here."

Viva looked at her with her head cocked to one side when Calder whistled to her and then lay down in the sun in front of the barn under the antique sign. She was no fun, so Calder went up to Barbie's alone. Barbie wanted to wait till Randy got through mowing someone's lawn, and it was perfectly clear that she wouldn't want Calder there when Randy came. Barbie said she had dated a year, but never seriously until this summer.

"See you," Calder said.

There were people at the tennis court back of the Inn. Maybe if she took her racquet and went over there and sat, somebody would ask her to play. But she'd have to hang around a long time first, and if they were couples they wouldn't want her anyway. But she wasn't bad. Dad said she was getting better all the time.

The main street stopped being a street at the last white house and became a dirt road, oiled down so it wasn't dusty, and ran straight up hill. Calder played a game: she walked as fast as she could without stopping until she got to the first level place, even though she was breathing so hard Dad would say her breath was coming in short pants. Then she took the next steep stretch without stopping. She'd try it on her bicycle next time so she could sail all the way down, even if she had to walk most of the way up.

At the top there was a big old empty house. She thought of sitting on the front porch to rest, but the house looked too deserted behind its bare windows. There was an electric light on by the door that made it look all the emptier. Anyway, the road led into a cool green tunnelly place here

with trees on either side, and the sun was greeny-gold, so she went on. Woods crowded up to the stone wall, and when she stood on the wall, the woods smelled damp. White toadstools stuck up in a circle as though elves had just had a meeting. Ferns grew all over the place. She jumped down and went on until the road came out into the sun again.

It was nice being up above the village by herself. If Mardie's house were only up here instead of down on the common, it would be more fun. On the other side of the wall, a yellow-green meadow spread out until it reached another wall and more woods. You couldn't get very far from woods any place you went, or from stone walls, either. That was what made Vermont so different from California—but then, everything was so terribly, dreadfully different.

Calder managed to slip under the barbed wire that ran above the wall without getting snagged. She wondered what she would come to if she crossed the meadow and went through the woods. They seemed to climb a hill, too.

A dog barked from the farmhouse up the road, but she couldn't see him. Then another dog joined in. Maybe she wasn't supposed to be in this field. The dogs must be shut up in that barn so they couldn't come at her—unless the farmer let them out, of course. The barking echoed to beat the band. How could the dogs tell she was crossing the field if they couldn't see her? She hadn't made any noise at all.

She stood still, expecting the owner of the dogs to appear suddenly and yell at her to get out of his field. Nobody came, but the dogs went on barking harder. She could hear them jumping up against the wall of the barn to try to get out. There must not be anybody at the farm, so the dogs were guarding it. She began to run. Then, without any warning at all, the solid ground turned into squshy swamp, and her feet went into muck above the top of her sneakers. Mud stuck to her ankles and felt gucky. It was cold, too. The ground ahead looked firm, so she took a jump, but only sank in deeper. As though the dogs could hear the squshy sound, their barking grew more frantic. She felt as if she were fleeing from the police in a movie she had seen one time. The police had dogs to follow the criminal. But why didn't the dogs lose her scent in the swamp? Or did you have to go through running water the way the criminal in the movie had?

The ground ahead sloped up to the stone wall just at the edge of a wood. Calder ran as fast as she could with the swamp sucking at her ankles until she reached the higher ground. As suddenly as it had begun, the barking stopped. The stillness was delicious. She didn't climb the wall for a minute for fear of spoiling that lovely silence. The trees on the other side were mostly pine and grew so close together the sun only trickled through. The piney ground was all up hill. She wondered how far you had to climb. She didn't want to go back and start the dogs barking again, and she certainly didn't want to go through that gucky field. Maybe she could see another road leading back to the village if she went to the top of the hill.

When she climbed the wall, she knocked a stone off; it didn't make a very loud sound, but it was enough to start the dogs barking again. Once she was inside the wood on the dry pine needles, the barking stopped.

The needles made the ground slippery. Branches caught at her hair. She gathered her hair up with one hand and tucked it in the neck of her turtle-necked shirt; that was better. The woods climbed ahead of her as far as she could see, and she wondered if she could get lost. But, of course, all she had to do was to come back down until she reached the wall and cross the swampy ground to the road. She should have brought her girl-scout knife so she could make a blaze on a tree. She pulled off the red ribbon around her head and tied it on a branch of one of the pine trees.

A jay flew out of the tree right above her head with a hoarse warning screech that frightened her. A stick snapped. She thought she heard a footstep, but she couldn't see anything except tree-trunks, with the sun sliding between them in thin stripes of light. She stood still so long she could hear her heart beating. Maybe she had heard the thumps of her heart instead of a footstep. Ducking her head out of the way of the low branches, she pushed on, not bothering to move quietly. You scared yourself if you were too quiet in the woods.

It was farther than she had thought to the top of the hill, and not much fun with the trees growing so close. She stumbled into some blackberry bushes and backed out, turning over to the right where there was a little clear space. When she looked back to the red ribbon, she hadn't come as far as she had thought. She started on and stopped suddenly.

What was that in there between the trees? Something big and dark She took a cautious step. It was rock—a great, rounded rock, tilted forward as though it had been rolling and just come to a stop. It was enormous and stood all by itself, with the trees almost hiding it. The front of the rock jutted out over its base like a heavy bulging forehead. Calder walked slowly up to it; the rock was three times as tall as she was.

How did such a huge rock happen to be hidden in the center of the woods? Maybe the Indians knew about it and used it for a lookout before the trees were here. Maybe they had rounded it, except that it wasn't smooth any place; it was covered with scars. And the rock was a different color from most rocks; it was more greenish than gray—with rusty streaks on it.

She tried to find a place where she could climb up, but the rock bulged out from its base on every side, and there was no place to put your foot. She climbed out on a big bough of the pine tree that grew closest to the rock, getting her hands and shirt and jeans covered with pitch. When she swung one foot out she could just touch the rock, but she couldn't put her weight on it. There was a little place—maybe she could get a handhold if she could reach that high.

She slid down out of the tree and tried the rock again, clawing at the rough surface with her fingers. Her pitch-covered hands held better as she heaved herself up on the rock. She found the notch and dug her fingers into it, squirming against the rock until she could get one knee up, then the other. She scrambled over the side and managed to lie on the flat top. When she got to her feet, she felt as perched as the rock was, but there was lots of room on the top to walk around.

"I'm the King of the Mountain!" she shouted out,

17

stretching her arms and looking down over the tree tops below her to a little speck of the squshy meadow she could see between them. But the sound of her own voice was too loud. The light in here was green and shadowy. She felt, suddenly, as though someone were watching her, and dropped to her knees, looking hard through the dark branches. A little breeze drifted through the wood, slapping together the leaves of the big beech tree near the rock and dying away in a kind of sigh. A shiver ran over her skin, and she sat a minute, not daring to move, listening. But it was nothing but the wind.

Calder slid down the side of the rock and jumped. The light was gloomy down here, with the dark rock so high and huge behind her and the trees closing her in, watching her. She swallowed and heard the sound of her own swallowing underneath the sighing of the wind through the wood. There *was* something secret about the rock hidden in here. She would come back again in the bright morning light, not late in the afternoon. And she wouldn't tell anyone about this place, not Barbie, not even Gran.

When she looked at the pitch-smeared face of her watch, it was after five, so there was nothing to do but go back the way she had come, through the swamp and the noise of those barking dogs. She looked back once; the great rock was already hidden.

Calder began to run. As she got to the wall the dogs' barking rose so frantically she kept an eye on the barn to see if they were loose. Their barking hounded her all the way across the marshy meadow until she climbed the second wall and was on the road again. Maybe the dogs and the swamp were there to guard the rock, to keep people from finding it. Maybe the rock was really enchanted!

Having a secret made a difference, Calder thought as she sat at dinner that night, listening to Mardie tell about Mother and how she was one of those women who was made for a career. "She's like me," Mardie said. Calder was wondering whether Mother had ever gone to the rock. But she didn't want to ask right out because she didn't want to say she had been there. And especially she didn't want to tell Mardie that she had been there all by herself. There was no use getting Mardie excited about her going off on the hills alone. She might tell her she couldn't. If Dad ever saw the rock, he'd make up wonderful stories about it.

"There are lots of rocks here, aren't there?" Calder said in a fine grown-up, conversational tone.

"I should say there are. Vermont is famous for its marble quarries and its granite. Wresting a living from this rocky soil is what has given Vermonters their strength of character."

Calder liked the word *wresting*; it sounded like a book word, and Mardie's voice sounded as if she were quoting something.

"And your roots come from this same soil, Calder. You must never forget that. Nothing can ever be too much for you. Just remember that your ancestor, Jonathan Calder, hewed his land out of the wilderness and cleared it of boulders and cobble stones and built himself a fine log house with his own hands!" Mardie's voice sounded as if she were giving a speech.

"I should think he would have built himself a stone house," Calder said.

"Why no—" Mardie hesitated. "I suppose it would have been hard to find the right kind of stones, and he wouldn't have had log plaster, I guess."

Calder wondered why there weren't any stone houses in the village after they did get plaster, but Mardie went on.

"And I suppose they wanted to use the wood of the trees they cut down when they cleared the forest. Calder, dear, are you happy here?"

Mardie jumped around so. Calder knew that Mardie wanted her to say she was. Mother had said to be thoughtful of Gran. "She's very lonely, yet she goes up there every summer and works hard at that little antique business. It's so wonderful for her to have you there." Calder didn't answer right off, but Mardie could see that she couldn't talk with her mouth full.

"Why Gran—Mardie, I mean, it's lovely here, but it's kind of quiet, and—and there isn't all that much to do."

"I know, Calder. It's quiet for me, too, and that's one of the reasons I run my antique shop. But the beauty and peace of the hills will grow on you, dear."

When Mardie stopped being so lively, she looked more like Mother, Calder thought.

"I wonder, Calder, if you would like to help me in the shop tomorrow? I could tell you about everything, and maybe I could even leave you in charge. There's an auction I want to go to next week. You're only twelve, but you're old for your age, living in that crazy household."

She *didn't* live in a crazy household, and Calder hated

Gran making horrid remarks like that. Home was loads more fun than being here, and she had friends and the swimming pool, and they went down to the ocean all the time, and Dad and she had jokes. . . .

"O.K." she mumbled.

3

The boy, Walt Bolles his name was, had been cleaning out the cow stanchion when the dogs started barking. At first he went on working because the dogs always barked when anyone went by, day or night. They sounded like a whole pack of ferocious hounds and were enough to scare off any thieves or bums, which was why Aunt Lil had them there. Brownie was nine years old and blind in one eye. Fido was part shepherd and part German police by his looks, and only three. Walt hated their being shut up in the feed room all the time, but when he asked Aunt Lil if they couldn't run free sometimes, she said to leave 'em right where they were, that they were the only protection she had up here.

Usually they quieted down after people passed. They

didn't mind cars so much, just the sound of feet or voices or maybe the scent of people. Most of the time, nobody did go by on foot. Today, the dogs were keeping it up; Fido barked so hard that he slavered at the mouth and jumped at the window. Brownie stood with his legs braced and his head lifted and took up whenever Fido stopped for breath. Their barking got louder, and they sounded as if they'd tear down the barn wall. Walt hung the shovel back on its hook, and climbed up on a sack of feed to see out of the dusty window.

A girl was crossing the meadow, running as fast as she could. He grinned when he saw her sink in and have to pull her foot out of the mud. That slowed her down! Where did she think she was going, anyway? She didn't even look over at the barn. He didn't think she was from around here—prob'ly one of the summer kids, trying to be a hippie, wearing torn-off jeans and a crazy colored shirt and her hair all loose down her back. If she went up in the woods, she'd get that long hair of hers caught on the branches.

Somebody must have told her about the rock, so she thought she could find it by herself. He didn't want summer people trailing up to the rock. It was on his father's and his aunt's land, so it belonged to him, too. Those darned postcards that they sold in the village were what sent folks to try to find it. But the picture on the cards was taken years before he was even born when the rock stood on a bare hillside. Now the hill was all grown up to woods, and you had to hunt to find it. He was glad of it, too. It wasn't any ordinary rock. It'd been dropped there by a glacier, and there wasn't another rock that big anywheres around. It looked as if it would keep on rolling if you just gave it a little push, but it was so heavy it was there to stay till kingdom come. It must have dug in as deep as an iceberg. He wished he could see how much of it was buried.

She was still going! Walt decided to sneak around and go up his special way and see if she found the rock. He'd never seen a girl go up there alone before. The dogs were barking worse than ever as he slipped out through the side door of the barn, but it wasn't any use to tell 'em to shut up.

He could skin up the hill a long sight faster than any girl could and keep out of sight all the way. Even he had to keep a sharp lookout for the rock; it had the darndest way of hiding. And then, all of a sudden, there it was, right in front of you. It always gave him a funny feeling.

When Walt came in sight of the rock, he could tell the girl was climbing the wall, because she knocked a stone off. That really made the dogs go wild! He climbed up in the beech tree that grew in the midst of the pines, pretty close to the rock, and got way up high in a good crotch of a limb so he could watch and not be seen. Then he remembered he had on his old ragged red shirt. He took it off and wadded it up and hid it on the other side of the tree for fear it would show. He was plenty hot from running, and it felt good to lie against the bark with his back bare. He took care to brush the loose pieces of twig off the limb, so nothing would fall down and give him away.

She was hunting for the rock, all right, because she stood still, looking around. The dogs stopped barking, and it was so quiet his own breathing sounded loud. If she weren't so close, he'd like to give his crow cry and scare the daylights out of her. He bet she wouldn't ever try to come up here again after that! She'd got her hair caught on a branch, just as he knew she would. She had to stop and pull it loose. She was stuffing the whole mess in the back of her shirt. It must be itchy.

What the heck was she doing now? She'd pulled the red ribbon off her hair—Oh, she was tying it on a branch as a marker. If she thought he was going to let it stay there, she had another think coming. You had to hunt for the rock every time; he wouldn't ever mark it for himself even. That girl was as bad as the lady in town who wanted him to cut a path and make blazes so the summer people could find the rock; said she'd pay him for it. He'd said he might, but he sure as heck never was going to do it! Kids in the village didn't come up here hardly at all. Most of 'em didn't think it was anything much. He never said anything about it to anybody either. He wanted it for his own. His father knew about it. The last time he went to see him at the Vet'rans' Hospital, he asked his father if he remembered it, because his father'd been born on this farm. His father knew all about it; he'd even slept underneath it once't. The rock meant more to him after that. If he saw anyone coming up here, he always kept an eye on 'em. Wasn't anybody going to get to carve his name on it while he was around. There were some initials and hearts with an arrow through 'em; that silly sort of stuff, but they were getting wore off. One had a date '' '89'' by it.

The girl had spotted it! He could tell because she sort of stiffened and stopped in her tracks. The rock reared up so big and sudden, it scared you the first time; it always gave you a little start, even after you'd seen it lots of times. It was like some heathen tomb hid away in the jungle.

Now she was so close to the tree that he could drop a twig down on her. She was walking around the rock. Funny a girl would come up here alone. Girls always seemed to be with other girls, or boys, of course. Not him; he didn't go for girls.

She was actually trying to figure how to get up on it! He'd like to take a flying leap and land on the rock in front of her. That would send her kiting. But the limb he was on wasn't that close, and unless he got started right, he might not make it. The first time he came up here, he found a broken-down ladder that someone had nailed together and

26

leaned against the rock. He got rid of that fast enough, broke it into pieces and threw them away. He didn't want to make it that easy.

She won't make it by climbing that pine tree, the crazy thing! Look at her swinging her leg, trying to touch it! Now she's given that up; she's going to try the rock again. She went to the right place, but you had to give a good jump and hoist yourself up by your arms; girls weren't any good at pulling themselves up by their arms. He could give her a boost if he jumped down there, but then she'd know he'd been watching her all the time and go back down to the village and blab about it. He was so stiff that he had to move, and a piece of bark dropped to the ground with a loud enough sound for anyone to hear it, but she was too busy trying to get up on the rock to pay any attention.

She'd got her fingers in that little notch. She was hanging on for dear life—she'd got a knee up. There she was, standing on it!

"I'm the King of the Mountain!" she shouted out, holding her arms up in the air. What kind of a crazy business was that! He leaned a little closer to get a good look at her. She was squatting down looking toward his tree. He froze, but he could see her slide down off the rock and jump to the ground. She looked at the watch on her wrist and then took one more look at the rock and started to run back down toward the wall. Didn't even stop for her ribbon. He could tell when she was in the meadow by the dogs. Brownie made a worse noise than Fido, because his voice was higher.

Walt jumped down from the tree and climbed the rock

27

himself. He stretched his arms up high and called out softly in a girl-kind of voice, "I'm the King of the Mountain!" You did feel like that, standing up here. He slid off the rock and beat it for home, forgetting his shirt till he was halfway there.

4

Calder wished she could sell something by herself. Most of the people who came to the antique shop said, "Thank you, my dear, we're just looking at all these lovely old things." Or they said, "We'll come back again when Mrs. Calder is here." And then there were the boring long stretches when no one came, and she sat in the wing chair that was marked "Elderly," because Mardie couldn't be *absolutely* sure of the date. "For I'm always completely frank and honest, Calder. That's why people come to my shop year after year. But you can say that it's *probably* late 18th century." Calder hoped nobody would buy it, because it was the only comfortable chair to sit on in the whole shop. She kept *Wind in the Willows*, which she had brought from home, hidden under the cushion.

It was rather nice out here in the barn with the doors wide open. Cars slowed down when the people in them saw the sign, and she played a game deciding whether they'd stop. Sometimes, she could see them arguing about it, and then they'd drive on fast.

When the elderly man came up the walk, Calder stood up and said, "Good afternoon," as Mardie said to do. "Don't ever hurry them, no matter how long they take, and treat them as though they were your guests dropping in."

"And it is a good afternoon," the man said, really looking at her. Mostly, people's eyes were darting all over the shop, so they hardly noticed her. "I wonder if you would have a cane, by any chance? I really would like a handmade one, an old-time staff to lean on. I was in here the other day, but I forgot to ask Mrs. Calder."

"I don't know. I'll look," Calder said. But she had gone over everything with Mardie, and she was pretty sure there weren't any canes.

"We'll both look," the man said.

They began on opposite sides of the barn. "My Grandmother's specialty is old glass," Calder said, looking at the sun coming through the shelves of colored glass in the window. Splotches·of color lay on the planks of the barn floor, and a yellow-green spot rested on the gentleman's bald head as he stood looking up at the barn rafters. It made him look jollier, Calder thought. The yellow-green was vaseline glass, Mardie said. The name wouldn't make you want to buy it, nor the color either. Cranberry glass sounded better and was prettier looking.

"What's that up there on those pegs?" The man pointed

to a stick lying close to one of the low beams. He had a nice laugh. "Unless my eyes deceive me, that is nothing more or less than a cane!"

Calder brought the footstool with the almost perfect needle-point top, except for a few moth-holes Mardie said to point out to anyone. But he wasn't tall enough to reach it.

"I think we can get it with this," he said, taking the rake that was supposed to be out of sight back in the corner. "Now, stand back, Jack Dalton!" A cane rolled off the pegs, and he caught it. "That is what I call an altogether elegant cane," he told her. "Exactly the sort of thing I had in mind." He fingered it carefully as though it were valuable. "Ash, I think. That ought to aid my doddering footsteps. What price do you ask for this fine example of folk art?"

31

Calder laughed, but he said, "No, I mean it. The carving is really very good." Mardie had said everything was marked, so she wouldn't have any trouble.

"Isn't there a sticker on it with the price?"

"The closest scrutiny reveals not a mark," the man said. "I want it, whatever the price. Suppose I take it and write my name down and come by tomorrow to pay for it. I'm staying at the Inn." Without waiting for her to agree, he wrote his name on the bill-pad on the high schoolmaster's desk that Mardie said she wouldn't sell for one cent less than three hundred dollars. His name was Binghampton Cooley.

Calder hesitated. "If you're coming here tomorrow, anyway, couldn't you wait and take the cane then?" And then, because she felt she might hurt his feelings, she said, "You look very honest, and I'm sure it would be all right, but my grandmother did tell me not to charge anything."

Mr. Cooley's smile made it all right. "As long as you think I have an honest look, I'm content, and you are entirely correct. I planned to take a little walk up one of these hills looking at rocks. I'm a superannuated geology professor, but this gives me an excellent reason for being lazy."

"And you don't really mind?" Calder asked anxiously.

"Not in the least. You are only doing your duty." He was fingering the head carved on the cane. "Would you say that was the head of a beagle or a spaniel?" They studied it together.

"Not a poodle," Calder said.

"Definitely not a poodle. I believe I prefer it to be a

beagle. I used to have one named Thucydides. He went with me on all my field trips.''

''That's a pretty long name to call.''

''Oh, I called him Thucy. And people used to get confused and think I was saying Lucy. Thucy got very much offended.'' He walked across the barn floor, in and out of the blocks of color, trying the cane. ''A cane gives a man a fine sense of importance, don't you think? Far from being superannuated, I feel positively dapper.'' He laid the cane across his arm, the head toward her. ''Keep it safely for me, Miss. . . .''

''Bailey. My name is Calder Bailey.''

Mr. Binghampton Cooley bowed. ''Good-by, Miss Calder Bailey.''

''You can just call me Calder,'' she told him.

She went back to her book thinking how pleased and surprised Mardie would be that she had sold something.

But Mardie said, ''Oh, Calder, you should have let Mr. Cooley take the cane!''

''You said not to charge anything.''

''Yes, I know, but someone like that. He's quite charming. I met him at the Inn at that cocktail party I went to.''

''He said he didn't mind at all.'' Calder was opening and closing the cover of the long-handled bed-warmer. How could you ever tell what Mardie meant?

''Don't fiddle with that, Calder. The catch isn't good. I just hope I sell it before it breaks. No, I'm sure he didn't mind, and he'll be back. He's really a very cultured person.''

Mr. Cooley didn't come the next morning, and at lunch Mardie asked Calder if she was sure she had been polite to him.

"Yes, I was, Grandmother! I told you he said he didn't mind and that I was only doing my duty."

"Well, if you used that tone of voice, you weren't being very polite."

Calder didn't answer. Three meals a day with Gran were a drag; she'd written Mother that. Mother had written back that she should just think of all the meals Gran had to eat alone. What was so bad about that? She would rather eat alone and get through quick; besides, she could read while she ate.

Mr. Cooley did come in the afternoon, finally. Calder saw him from the porch, but Gran was out in the shop, so she went on reading *Wuthering Heights*.

Then she heard Gran and Mr. Cooley coming toward the porch and wished she had escaped. She hoped Gran noticed that she got out of the swing and stood up; that ought to be polite enough for her. Most kids didn't.

"Ah, there's the young lady who helped me find the cane," Mr. Cooley said. But, of course, she hadn't; he had found it for himself. Grownups didn't tell things exactly. But he was nice, and she smiled at him. He had his cane.

"I've asked Mr. Cooley to have a glass of sherry, Calder, and I thought you would like to entertain him while I get it," Gran said in her company voice.

"Your grandmother tells me you come from southern California, Calder," he said, as he sat down.

"Yes, and I like it there," she said quickly, because

Gran was always saying it was the very last place in the world she'd ever want to live in.

Mr. Cooley laughed. "You know, I do, too. I lived and taught there for a good many years."

"You did!" Calder looked at him as if it should show in some way.

"Is that unbelievable?"

"I guess I just didn't expect to see anybody from California here."

"It's very different from New England, but it has its own beauty, if you can get away from its cities. But that's true of New England cities, too," Mr. Cooley observed. "They're not apt to be noted for their beauty anywhere."

"California has beauty," Calder said, and unexpectedly, her mouth trembled. She had to sniff loudly, but Mr. Cooley was filling his pipe and didn't notice. "Did you use to go to the ocean?" she asked.

"I lived in Santa Barbara. I used to go down to the ocean every day," Mr. Cooley said.

Calder clasped her arms around her knees and pulled them up to her chin in her excitement. "We lived eleven blocks from the ocean, but I used to ride down there all the time on my bike."

Gran came back with a tray, and little cucumber sandwiches, and the hand-blown sherry bottle with two little glasses, and a tall glass of grape juice for Calder. Calder's eyes went swiftly over the tray. She wondered how Gran had made six cucumber sandwiches and cut the bread rounds so fast.

"We've just been sharing our fondness for California,"

Mr. Cooley said.

"Well, I must admit that it leaves me very cold," Gran said in that hateful, superior tone of hers. "But, of course, I'm a New Englander, born and bred."

Calder waited to hear what Mr. Cooley would say. Her grape juice must have come out of the cupboard, because it wasn't really cold, and Gran hadn't bothered to put any ice cubes in it.

"My roots are here too, but so long ago that they hardly count," Mr. Cooley began, but Gran cut right in the way she did with Calder.

"Don't ever say that. They certainly do count. That's what I tell Calder."

"I suppose I just like the land, Europe as well as this country, so I never set one part over against another. Right now, I'm enjoying these hills."

Calder was disappointed that he couldn't stick up for California any better than that. She started into the house to get some ice for her grape juice, but she heard Mr. Cooley saying, "And I'm greatly interested in the rocks around here."

"There are certainly plenty of those!" Gran laughed her merry tinkling laugh that was nothing like Mother's big hearty laugh.

When Calder came back from the kitchen, moving her glass to make the ice cubes melt, Mr. Cooley was showing Gran a postcard. Gran had to get her glasses, which she never wore when company was there, so Calder went over to look at the card. Mr. Cooley handed it to her.

She stared at it, hardly believing what she saw. It was a picture of her rock! There was the place where she had climbed up, and there was the bulge she had walked under—only there were no trees around it. The rock on the postcard was just perched on a bare hill with the sky coming down all around it. But there was the same tilt; the rock on the card looked as though it would roll on down hill, even more than the rock in the woods, but there was no secret feeling about it.

"Here, Calder, let me see," Gran said, putting on her glasses with the blue frames. "Oh, yes indeed, I can tell you all about this rock. It's Serpentine rock. We used to go up there and take picnics when I was young. It was a great landmark. But the trees have grown up so terribly it's very hard to find. In fact, I'm trying to get a boy to make a good trail up to it because it *is* an attraction, and it would be a place for visitors at the Inn, like yourself, to go."

Calder listened to Gran with horror. She minded Gran's knowing all about her secret, and she hated the idea of a trail up to it.

"I saw this postcard at the Inn and asked the young man at the desk how I would get there, but he didn't seem to know," Mr. Cooley said. "It's an erratic boulder, of course, dropped by the glacier about two hundred and fifty thousand years ago, a rather impressive one."

Calder heard only the words "erratic boulder." Gran had said Dad was erratic.

"What road would I take to get up there?" Mr. Cooley asked.

"I'm afraid you would have a hard time finding it by yourself."

Calder almost said she had found the rock by herself, but something made her keep still.

37

"People are always going up there and coming back disappointed. It's up the road to the old town of Weldon, when it used to be on the hill instead of down here in the valley, whether to protect the settlement from the Indians or what, I don't really know. But there's a farmhouse up near the rock, on the road below it, that is; and there's a boy there who could probably take you to it. When you want to go, I would be glad to drive you up and get the boy to take you."

Mr. Cooley finished his second glass of sherry and set it down on the table. "Thank you. I think with my new cane I'll just walk up the road tomorrow and ask him, myself." Mr. Cooley looked over at Calder. "Maybe my fellow Californian here would go with me?"

"I'm sure Calder would love to go," Gran said. "Wouldn't you, dear? And then you could bring Mr. Cooley back here for supper."

Calder sat silent. She wasn't sure she wanted to go to her secret place with anyone. Her eyes met Mr. Cooley's. He was waiting for her to answer.

"O.K." she said, forgetting that Gran had asked her not to say O.K.

5

Mr. Cooley was waiting for her on the porch of the Inn when Calder came up the street. He looked younger then he had back at Gran's and awfully clean in his khaki shirt and trousers, and he wore a funny straw hat with a hole in it. He had his cane and a canteen on a strap over his shoulder, as though he were going on a real climb. If she had told him about the swamp, he might not have worn those clean desert boots. She felt a little guilty about that. She had worn her torn-off shorts and oldest sneakers.

"I've decided to name my staff Agassiz instead of Thucy," he told Calder, as they started up the road.

"It isn't as easy to say as Thucy."

"No, but we can call him Louie; Louie Agassiz. It's

quite an appropriate name, considering our expedition, because Agassiz was mightily interested in ice sheets that moved over the earth dropping boulders like ours in their path. In fact, he was the one who really proved that's the way they got here."

Calder didn't know that she liked his calling the rock "ours." It had been hers. He walked faster than she had expected he would, but he had to stop when the road got steep. He looked back at the village. "We'll have to admit that your Grandmother is right about its being pretty."

"Oh yes, it's pretty enough, and it's more fun when you get up on the hill outside of the village." She was trying to decide whether she should tell him she had already been to the rock. Wouldn't he be surprised! He didn't talk as much as most older people—Gran, for instance. They walked along in silence when they started on again, so she had plenty of time to make up her mind. As long as she didn't *say* she had already been to the rock, she still had a secret.

When they came to the cool green tunnelly place, Mr. Cooley stopped again. He sat down on the wall and took off his hat. It was funny; that was just about where she had stopped.

"It's hard for us desert rats to get used to all this damp green at first, isn't it?"

"I'm not a desert rat; Dad calls me a sea urchin. I'd rather have the sea than these woods, any day!"

He didn't answer right away; then he said, "But you have both now, haven't you? The sad thing would be if you'd never seen the ocean or never seen rolling green hills and woods like these."

"But I mean I'd rather be there, by the ocean. Right now."

"All you have to do is just sit still on that wall and think yourself there. It's not hard to do."

"You mean pretend."

"More than pretend; really feel yourself there. Tell me what color the ocean is today?"

To be polite, she sat on the wall and closed her eyes.

"You don't need to close your eyes. Look right through the woods and see the ocean."

He was a little nutty. "Well—it's deep blue, and tan where the waves come in on the sand. And the sand's almost white. . . ." She really could see it. "And when the waves roll back, there are dark wet scallops of sand, and some shells, and weeds and stuff. I've picked up so many shells that Mother said I had to stop bringing any more home."

"I know. I always come home with rocks in my pockets, and I had to stop that. Now I just go around with rocks in my head." He laughed. "You'll discover that." He got up and started on.

"Maybe nobody'll be at the farm."

"Your grandmother seems to think they're pretty sure to be there; this boy, anyway. He lives with his aunt, she tells me. I think your grandmother has lived here so long that she knows everyone around here and their habits. There's something to be said for that, Calder. You know, where we live, people haven't been there so long, and they move more often."

Calder scowled.

41

Mr. Cooley pointed Louie at a bronze plaque stuck to a big rock beside the road. Calder had missed that. It said that Weldon used to be up here, and it had numbers so you could hunt for the markers that told where the church used to be and the potash plant and even the houses of some of the people. Calder looked around trying to see a village way up here. She couldn't.

"It's hard to imagine a whole village making up its mind to move, isn't it?" Mr. Cooley asked. "Especially, when they had their houses and barns and gardens, and their fields were cleared and marked off by stone walls. I suppose that the few places that are still up here belonged to the die-hards who said, 'You can go if you want to, but we're going to damn well stay here.' You'll have to excuse my language, Calder."

"Oh, that's O.K. I'm used to it. Dad swears a lot. Mother does, too, sometimes. Maybe people do more in California."

"That's an interesting thought. But it's one of those dangerous generalizations that would have to be thoroughly investigated before you could state it as fact."

She wasn't quite sure about the word generalization, and she looked quickly at him to see if he was making fun of her, but decided he wasn't. He just didn't make any difference talking to grownups and not grownups, thank goodness! She might tell him, after all, before they got to the farm house and warn him about the dogs barking and the swampy ground. His shoes would be a mess when they got into the guck. They'd never really clean up right, either; Dad had some that hadn't. Maybe they could go down that old grassy road that must have been part of the old town and then cross over, but the dogs began barking. If they went up to the farm, she could see the dogs.

"They sound hospitable, don't they! Why don't you wait for me here."

She didn't, but she walked more slowly. Mr. Cooley went up the driveway to the house and knocked on the door. No one came. The dogs were really going wild. Somebody inside the barn told them to shut up, then the door at the side of the big door opened and a boy came out.

"Whaddya want?" He was skinny and pretty tall; taller than she was, and she was taller than most boys her age. His hair scraggled down to his shirt collar, and he wasn't very clean. He came as far as the road.

"How do you do. My name is Cooley." Mr. Cooley came back down from the porch to meet him. The dogs were jumping up against the side of the barn inside and barking so loud she had to go closer to hear what Mr. Cooley said, but she moved over to the side of the road so the boy didn't see her.

"I'm glad you're here to keep those watchdogs under control," Mr. Cooley said.

"They're O.K." the boy said. "They can't get out."

"Yes, I realize that, but they sound as though they might break the door down. My companion and I are interested in going up to that boulder we've heard about, Serpentine Rock, I believe you call it." The boy was looking down at the ground. Calder hoped he would say he didn't want to take them, and then she would step up and say she could find it.

43

"That barking makes conversation rather difficult; perhaps we could walk up the road a little way."

"They'll keep it up as long as you're on our land," the boy said. But as he turned to walk away from the barn with Mr. Cooley, he saw Calder. She guessed she scared him, just standing there.

"This is my friend," Mr. Cooley said. "Calder Bailey. I've promised to take her up to see the boulder, and I know she would be disappointed if we couldn't find it." Calder felt the boy looking right at her. He had dark brown eyes, really dark.

"The rock's up there in those trees. Anybody can find it if they look hard enough. Maybe she can skin up there an' find it for you!"

"I am sure that we can find the boulder if you don't care to help us," Mr. Cooley said. "You understand, I expect to pay for your time. I know wages are pretty high for the services of an experienced mountain guide."

Mr. Cooley's voice was cold as ice, Calder thought. She felt almost sorry for the boy. He was frowning a little and still looking at her. "Sure, maybe I could find it," she said. "If it's just up there in those woods."

"Would two dollars make it worth your while?" Mr. Cooley asked. The dogs' barking filled the whole valley from hill to hill, just as it had the other time. The boy's eyes moved back to Mr. Cooley.

"By the way, you didn't tell me your name," Mr. Cooley said. "Your name," he had to repeat.

"Walt. Walt Bolles." The boy darted another look at her, pushing the hair back from his face. "Yeah, I'll take you, but you'll have to get yourselves back; I can't stay up there. I got chores to do.''

"I should think we might be able to manage that, wouldn't you, Calder?''

The boy started over toward the wall. "You have to climb over the wall and watch out for the barbed wire.'' He held it down close to the stones so they could step over it. But when Mr. Cooley tried to hold down the wire for Walt, he stepped on it and took a leap into the meadow.

"Couldn't those dogs go with us, since you're along?'' Mr. Cooley asked. "I feel like a trespasser with all that din.''

"Nope. We keep 'em shut in. They stay here to take care of the place. Watch you don't sink in the mud; it's kinda swampy in here,'' he added as Mr. Cooley pulled his foot out of the mud with a squshing sound.

"Thank you for your warning,'' Mr. Cooley told him. "Would it be any firmer walking across to that farther field?''

"You can if you want. This is the shortest way.''

"If they make a trail up to the boulder, I trust they take the longer way,'' Mr. Cooley said, holding up Louie to see how deep the mud was.

"Who said anyone's goin' to make a trail up here? This is our land.''

"I heard that certain public-spirited townspeople would like to have a trail so that the town's visitors could see such a national monument. Geology students would be interested. Perhaps you could charge them something for the privilege of visiting your land.''

45

Mr. Cooley's voice could get real thin and sharp. The boy got it, too. Calder saw the red creep up into his hair.

"We don't want people tracking through our meadow. An' we don't want their money, either."

"I see. I should think the baying of the hounds might pretty well discourage them."

"It don't. They come anyhow, but at least they can't come up here without our knowing it. Look at that! Somebody's been up here an' tied a piece of red cloth on that tree for a marker. Not asking or anything!"

Calder had already spotted her red ribbon tied to the tree just the other side of the next wall. The boy—Walt —yanked it angrily off the branch and stuffed it in his pocket. Calder was thankful that she had her hair in pigtails today with elastic bands around them. Mr. Cooley held down the barbed wire that ran above this wall, too, with his cane. "You see, Calder, Louie can be very handy." Then, turning to the boy, he said, "This cane of mine is named Louis Agassiz after a famous geologist, who considered that the whole world was his to explore and study." The boy jumped over the wire and went on ahead.

"It's slippery on the pine needles," he called back down to them.

"Thank you," Mr. Cooley said. "The dogs bark until you're over the wall. Once you've come that far, they give up. I must say the stillness is a blessed relief."

"If I let 'em loose, they'd follow anyone up here fast enough and drive 'em out."

"How fortunate for us that you saw fit to guide us instead of turning the dogs on us. Let's stop here before we go on.

46

It's steeper than I would have expected." Mr. Cooley sat down on the ground with his cane between his knees.

The boy made no answer. He just stood leaning against a tree as though what they did was no concern of his. Calder went up a little farther, looking through the shadowy green for the first sight of something gray. The rock must be close. Those trees looked just like the ones around the rock, but when she got up to them, there was no sign of the rock. Even with the three of them, there was that same funny feeling in here, a feeling of being watched. Maybe she was too far to the left; she never could tell directions. Would that be east? The trees grew too close together in here to see what the sun was doing. She saw the boy watching her as she came back. Could he have seen her from the barn the other day? He'd said no one could come up here without his knowing it. Maybe he had been in the barn all that time. If he was, he probably thought she hadn't found it, and that was the reason she'd come back up here with Mr. Cooley and wanted him to show them. Well, she'd let him know she had found it. Only how could she prove it?

"The rock must be . . ." She changed her sentence to a question. "Is the rock close to where we are now?"

Walt was as slow as Mr. Cooley sometimes was in answering. Finally he said, "Folks think there isn't anything to finding it once they've seen it, but they're wrong!" His eyes had a kind of glint in them. "You're close enough to throw a cat and hit it, an' you can't even see it! Now I've brought you this far, you have to spot it by yourselves."

Mr. Cooley seemed not to hear him. He was studying the

47

postcard with the picture of the great rounded boulder perched on an open hillside. "I suppose this picture must have been taken about thirty years ago, judging by the boles of some of these pines and that beech tree over there. Certainly a good example of the wilderness taking back its own." He stood up. "Walt, if you're our guide, why must we find it for ourselves?"

The boy hunched one shoulder in a shrug. " 'Cause you do, that's all."

"Well, Calder, suppose we spread out a little. You keep to that side of this tree, and I'll take the other. Walt, you can tell us if we go too far afield, I trust. I gather that you take a very dim view of outlanders like us getting a glimpse of your rock, but don't let us walk a mile or so before you call us back."

For the first time, Walt smiled. His whole face changed. "It'll take you three minutes flat, unless you're blind. You gotta keep your eyes peeled. If you loan me that watch, I'll time you."

"That's a deal." Mr. Cooley slipped his watch off his wrist and handed it to Walt. "When we see it, we'll call out." The watch was an elaborate affair with separate dials to tell direction and the day of the year, besides the time. Walt had never seen anything like it. As they went off, Walt's head was bent over the watch.

Again the woods were quiet. Their feet on the thick pine needles made no sound. Calder went to the right, but she had a feeling that the rock was the other way. She could see Mr. Cooley's bald head moving through the trees. He stopped suddenly and held up his hand. He didn't call. She went to him. Then she saw it, too, just as she had that other time. A gray shadow at first, blocking the space between the trees, but it was no shadow. You couldn't get through it. Mr. Cooley reached out and touched her arm, and they went up to it. He laid his hand on the rough, scarred surface, looking up at it without saying a word. Then, just as she had done, he walked around it. Calder moved toward the front where the great rock tilted forward, and the bulge of it made an overhang you could stand under. Now she was glad she hadn't said she had been here before.

Mr. Cooley came around the side of the rock to her. "It seems much larger hidden in here than out in the open in the picture. I was startled, coming on it so suddenly."

"Hey, I thought you were going to call when you found it!" Walt appeared beside them.

"I forgot all about that, Walt, when I saw the rock. It has a kind of presence, hiding here in the woods."

Walt grinned. "Almost scared you, didn't it? It isn't anything but an old rock, but you don't know it's going to be there like that. That's why you gotta come on it by yourself. If there was a trail to it an' a marker an' all, it wouldn't be nothing, hardly." The surly note had disappeared from his voice long since. Now he sounded almost excited.

Mr. Cooley looked at him. "I believe you're right. The rock has taken on a kind of mystery because it's hidden in here."

"I don't want people coming up here an' having picnics and leaving their old beer cans around. Nor a picnic table, like a woman in town wants, either."

Calder thought of Mardie saying they used to come for picnics. Of course, Mardie wouldn't bring any beer cans along, but she'd like having a table here.

"I wonder how far the boulder traveled," Mr. Cooley said.

"Can't you see it rolling!" Calder laughed. "If it rolled down on your barn, it would smash it into matchsticks," she said to Walt.

"There weren't any human beings around to see it roll," Mr. Cooley went on. "It would have been part of the glacial drift picked up by a great ice sheet two hundred and fifty thousand or so years ago when the Siberian winter, as Louis Agassiz called it, covered the world. This boulder was broken off from some ledge and rounded by dragging it all this way. That's how it acquired all those glacial scrapings.

"But why do you figure it stopped *here* in our pasture?" Walt asked.

"It just came to a stop. All the gravel that came with it helped to stop it."

"Tell him the book name of it, Mr. Cooley," Calder said.

"The name? Oh, I said it was known as an erratic boulder because it was moved from its rightful place. Another name for it is lost rock, because it's lost from its parent lode."

"Some people are erratic," Calder said gravely.

Mr. Cooley chuckled. "Yes, Calder, some people are like erratic boulders. Maybe it's a good thing, too; but not easy on the person who is one."

"Less he can hide himself like this rock," Walt said. "Here's your watch; it's some watch!" He went over and hoisted himself against the rock until he could get his fingers in the notch and gave a mighty pull. He hoped *she* noticed that he didn't have to squirm on his stomach and kick around the way she did. But once he was up, he said to her,

"Here, I'll give you a hand."

She just stood there, looking up at him.

"Come on," he urged. "You can make it, if Mr. Cooley will give you a push."

"Calder, step on my hand and then take hold of Walt's," Mr. Cooley directed. "Why, you're a regular monkey," he said, as she put her foot on his hand, but sprang up on the rock without taking hold of Walt's proffered hand at all.

"Louie can't help me here." Mr. Cooley laid his cane down and scrambled up, but he pulled hard on Walt's hand.

"Say, you're pretty good!" Walt said.

Maybe it was Mr. Cooley's buying a cane that made him seem so old that day he came into the shop, Calder thought. He didn't seem ancient; he seemed kind of springy.

"Oh, I've done considerable climbing in my day, mostly on rocks, too."

The three of them stood on the boulder, well above the tops of some of the pines below them. The tilt of the rock hid the ground in front, so they seemed poised on a ball in green space.

"Look, there's a seat in the rock!" Calder seated herself gingerly in the cut-out hollow, hanging her legs over the front, her back to the others. "This is like a castle hidden in here, protected by a moat; only this moat's a squishy meadow. And those dogs are fierce hounds that are really prisoners changed by the evil sorceress of the castle."

Walt was looking at her when Calder turned around.

"Do you think the sorceress is apt to appear suddenly out of the rock and change us?" Mr. Cooley asked.

"No," she said slowly. "There couldn't be anything evil

53

about the rock." She looked through the sun-streaked woods, down through the openings in the trees to the meadow. It was hard to find a place for the evil creature. "Maybe the dogs are the evil creatures."

"Brownie and Fido aren't evil," Walt objected, and Calder collapsed into silence.

Mr. Cooley was examining the deep scars on the rock's surface. "You see, they show the same direction. Rocks have a great deal to tell us if we learn to read them. The earth itself is only a larger ball of rock, like this one, partly covered by water and surrounded by air, and every rock is a piece of the world that was here long before you were and will be after you."

His class of two was silent, staring at the rock. Then Walt jumped up and waved his arms above his head. "I'm the King of the Mountain!" he called out in a high, girlish voice.

Calder turned her head around so quickly that her braids bobbed; her face flushed red, her eyes glared at him. He had been hidden somewhere up here, watching her! Sneaking around spying on her! And he knew that was her ribbon when he called it an old red rag. Walt slid down over the side of the rock out of sight.

"You can get yourselves back, I guess. I got chores to do," he called up to them as he started off down the hill without looking back.

"Here, wait a minute, Walt. I owe you something," Mr. Cooley called. But Walt was running down the hill.

"I don't want anything," he called back. "But don't go telling folks how to find the rock."

54

The dogs gave only a yelp or two as he crossed the meadow. "How would they know it's Walt?" Calder asked, her face still flushed and resentful.

"I don't know. He's on odd lad," Mr. Cooley said, "but he has a spark when you get through to him. I like him. He really feels that rock belongs to him."

Calder made no answer.

Of course, bringing Mr. Cooley back to dinner was only Gran's way of speaking, and not true at all. Because he had to stop at the Inn and change his clothes and his muddy boots, and Calder had to bathe and get into a dress.

"I know that out in California your mother lets you come to the table in old shorts and even bare feet, but not here!" Gran said.

So Calder bathed and changed and brushed her hair out, but it was squiggly because of being braided so tightly and didn't fall straight and smooth. As she was tying a navy blue ribbon around her head, she thought she might just ask that Walt Bolles to kindly give back her red one!

Neither she or Mr. Cooley said very much about Walt at dinner. She certainly wasn't going to talk about the sneaky thing, and Mr. Cooley only said they found him and that he seemed a bright boy. He didn't mention how rude he was.

"He hasn't grown up here," Mardie said. "He just came to live here with his aunt, I understand, when his father was taken sick. I'm going up to see him one of these days and find out why he hasn't done anything about the trail I asked him to make. You know, it would be a chance for him to earn a little money, but I presume he's shiftless, like so

55

many of the young boys. You can't count on them to do anything!"

"Did his aunt give permission for the trail to be made?" Mr. Cooley asked, as he cut into the lemon meringue pie that Mardie prided herself on.

"I think Mrs. Canby spoke to her about it, but why should she mind?"

"Well, I just thought that Vermonters were rather fond of keeping fences up around their property, and I find a good many places posted against trespassers."

"We could have a gate made, of course, and put up a sign saying that it was private property and that the gate must be kept closed."

Calder ate in silence. How horrid it would be to have people trailing up to the rock. That was the only thing she liked about that boy: that he didn't want people to go up there.

"There must be springs in the meadow between the road and the wood; it's a regular swamp," Mr. Cooley said, dropping the subject of the trail.

But Mardie was busy with the coffee tray. The living room always seemed cold to Calder. The braided rugs weren't fluffy under your bare feet like the big orange and red rug on the living room floor at home, and instead of a big squashy couch there was a sofa so slippery you had to sit up straight to stay on it. The wallpaper was a pale blue with gold figures on it, and there seemed to be yards and yards of white woodwork and then white doors with funny brown doorknobs. Instead of great big green plants standing in stone jars on the floor, there were stingy little pots of

56

African violets on the window sill. Calder liked the room only when there was a fire on the hearth.

Mardie settled herself in a straight chair that matched the sofa, with the coffee tray in front of her on a one-legged, tippy little table. Calder passed the coffee cup to Mr. Cooley and took one herself, though she didn't really like the taste of coffee, but then she would go off up to her own room and start reading *Great Expectations,* which was next on her school reading list. She tried to think of an expectation for herself. Going back home, she guessed.

"What would be perfectly wonderful, Mr. Cooley," Gran was saying, "and a real contribution, would be for you to write about Serpentine Rock. You know, tell how it was brought down by a glacier, and how many years ago it probably was, and something about the kind of rock it is."

Mr. Cooley looked positively startled, Calder thought. "Anyone can find out about a boulder like that in an elementary geology textbook," he said.

"But they wouldn't, don't you see? And they wouldn't know what a—a phenomenon it is and how worthwhile to go up there to see it. I was thinking that we could have a little folder printed. Lucia Ingalls comes here in the summer to paint, and I think I could get her to do some nice little sketches. Oh, we'd have it very well done—two tones, perhaps, and sell the folders for the Development Society."

Mr. Cooley was filling his pipe. Calder finished drinking the bitter stuff, and put her cup back on the tray. Mardie nodded toward Mr. Cooley's cup, so she took it to be refilled. She would have gone upstairs then, but she wanted to hear Mr. Cooley say he wouldn't write any such thing about the rock.

He was so slow in answering, Mardie went on, "For instance, the rock itself, I remember, looks just like any big rock, but I've seen pieces of it polished until they look just like green marble. Calder, go up to your grandfather's secretary in the upstairs hall and see if there isn't a piece of rock in the cupboard above the desk part. John wasn't interested in rocks so much as in polishing them and seeing how the colors came out. He had all the equipment."

Calder had to stand on a chair to reach the top shelf, and when she leaned against the cupboard, it wobbled and everything in it rattled. The desk and the top part with the glass doors came in two parts, like the gravy dish and tray that Gran was always warning her about. In the cupboard were stuffed birds, a big conch shell, and an old revolver. She held the shell up to her ear a long moment to hear the faint sound of the ocean in it. She laid it on the desk to carry into her room. And then she found the triangular-shaped green piece of rock that really did look like marble. Calder forgot to close the cupboard doors and ran all the way downstairs, jumping the last two steps.

"Could this really be from our boulder, Mr. Cooley?"

Mr. Cooley turned the piece of rock over in his hand, holding it under the light so that it shone with a deep green lustre.

"It most certainly is," Mardie said. "John hammered it off, himself. It is beautiful, isn't it!"

"Yes, this is Serpentine," Mr. Cooley said. "Verde antique, that you find used on the walls of public buildings, is a form of serpentine."

"But I thought our rock was rare and brought down specially in that ice sheet?"

Mr. Cooley laughed. "On order? As a matter of fact, there's a vein of serpentine running down from Canada. The glacier broke off our boulder and swept it down here. It's almost beyond imagining," he said, turning to Mrs. Calder, "in a world so cold no animal life survived, the glacier hollowed out these rounded valleys and left the boulders it dragged with it scattered all through this country."

All night, Calder had dreams. Once she was sliding down some long slope and came to a stop only at the end of a precipice, with her feet pushed against the foot of her bed.

6

When neither Calder nor the old man came back up the hill all the next week, Walt wondered if the girl was mad at him for yelling out that he was the King of the Mountain. Girls got mad easy, or hurt; that was worse. It worried him some.

But why should they come again? Folks only wanted to see the rock once. And she'd been up here twice. He couldn't get why she didn't take the old man up there, herself; or why she didn't tell him she'd been there. And not saying a word when he took her ribbon off the tree, and asking if they were getting close, as though she'd never been up here before! What was the big idea?

The old man had said that about the rock's having a presence, and he'd liked the way they'd both been so still when they first spotted it, but the rock didn't really *mean* anything to them; not like it did to him. It was the only darn thing on the farm that he really cared about.

Walt was eating supper with his aunt at the kitchen table when he got the idea of going down and taking the girl's ribbon back to her. Maybe he'd tell her he was only kidding when he yelled that. You did feel like the King of the Mountain when you stood up on the rock, with the trees going down the hill in front of you. The next thing he knew, he was saying to his aunt that he was going to ride down to the village and see if there was ball practice.

"I thought practice was on Thursday night." Aunt Lil's eyes were sharp, looking across at him. "I don't want you going down and hanging around the store or some place, getting into devilment."

"They couldn't tell for sure when it was going to be, and, of course, nobody'd bother to come way up here to let me know." That was the truth.

Mrs. Bolles supposed the boy did feel left out of things, living way up here, when he'd always lived in town; but she wasn't used to boys, and it made her nervous waiting for him to get back. "It'll be dark as pitch tonight if you stay late. It's clouding up. If you ride your bicycle, you're likely to go head over heels."

"I've got a light on it," he said. "It's a super one, an' spreads all over the road." Aunt Lil was funny; she always acted as if she didn't want him to go places, but she didn't really say he couldn't. When he did things, like fixing the hinge on the screen door and straightening out the mess of tools in the barn, she never really said thank you. Her eyes

61

went over the job to find something wrong with it, and then if it was all right, she'd nod and tighten her mouth and think of something more he could do. Folks in town must think she was queer, staying up here alone, an' keeping a cow, an' driving the old '42 Ford they'd had when Uncle Nate was living. Dad said her living alone up here made her the way she was, keeping those dogs shut up in the barn for protection. Sometimes, he thought she was half-scared of them, herself. "But she means well," Dad had said. "You get along with her."

So he did. But he didn't like living here with her. Dad said it wouldn't be for long; only until he got well.

"Well, you can go, but if there isn't any practice, you come right back home, Walt."

"Maybe I'll go to the library; it's open tonight." His aunt didn't know that he wasn't on the team, that it didn't matter to them whether he got there for practice or not, unless too many kids were away. He wasn't too good at it, even though he practiced throwing balls at the back of the barn and catching them. The dogs had gone wild when he first did it. They were getting used to it now.

Getting out of the house at night felt good, better than sitting at the kitchen table reading, with Aunt Lil sitting there always figuring things on a pad of paper. He gathered speed, whirling through the dark dungeon of trees, with the breeze on his face and coming through his shirt. He hit the places hard where the road went up in little humps, and let his bike plunge down on the other side of them. There were only three houses on the way, summer places, all fixed up fancy. The Sterns, who had the big house at the top of the

62

hill, were in Europe, Aunt Lil said, but they left a light on day and night. It looked silly in the daytime and lonesome at night. When the road smoothed out, his tires made a smacking sound as they whirled down the hill. He bet she'd be scared riding down through here at night. Funny to have a last name for your first name. He wouldn't call her that when he saw her. He wouldn't call her anything.

Walt looked between the houses to the ball ground. They were out there all right, but they had enough kids. He'd just sit there and not get a chance to play. Last time he only got to play for a minute.

The Inn was all lighted up; folks were still eating in the dining room, and rocking on the porch, and walking around. It was a real swell place. He rode by slowly, but he didn't see Mr. Cooley. That old man sure knew a lot about rocks. He'd like to see him again. Funny guy, giving his cane a name like that.

Walt wasn't quite sure where the girl lived. The store was still lighted, so he dropped his bicycle against the long steps and went in. A man from the city, he could tell, was leaning on the counter talking to the store-keeper. They both looked at him as he opened the door, so he had to speak up.

"Say, I wondered, can you tell me where the Calder place is?"

"Third house down on the other side of the common," the store-keeper told him.

"Thanks," Walt said, and then because he felt he ought to say something more, he added, "I got an errand there."

He spotted the house right away, so close to the street it wouldn't take more than six steps to be on the front step, but there were bushes in front of it. The place was all lighted up, with a light out on the side porch, but you couldn't see anything because of the screens and the vines all over. He rode his bicycle slowly along the walk in front of the house. She must be out on the porch. He could hear people talking. A woman laughed, and then a man. He held the bike still.

"Calder's getting very good at keeping shop for me," he heard the woman say.

He waited to see if he could hear Calder. If she was there, she didn't say a word. Walt wheeled on past the house and saw the barn with a sign that said "Antiques," hanging out on an iron bracket. If they had a shop, maybe the girl couldn't get away often, and that was why she hadn't been back. He rode on around the whole common. Nice having that kind of park down here, with white houses sitting all around it. When he came back around, he could hear them still talking and laughing out there and the sound of dishes. They must be eating their supper on the porch. It looked pretty fancy, what he could see. He tried to hear if the man's voice was Mr. Cooley's, but he didn't think so.

Then he saw Calder. She opened the screen door to let a silly little poodle-dog out. She was in a light dress, and her hair was hanging down smooth to her shoulders, like the first time he saw her. She had a blue ribbon around her head.

"Here, Viva. Come on, Viva," she said to the dog. She was coming out on the stone steps, close enough so he could have called to her. He could say, "Hi!" real quiet. "I brought your hair-ribbon." But he didn't.

She stood there as if she didn't care if the dog came right

away or not. But she looked differ'nt in a dress, with the light shining on her hair like that. Pretty. He couldn't get out a word or make a noise so she'd hear him. He hoped the dog would run off, and she would have to chase it, but instead the silly thing trotted back up to the step, and the girl opened the door and went inside after him.

Walt sat on his bicycle behind the bushes, just as he'd hidden up at the rock. He might hang the red ribbon on the door knob, and she'd know he'd brought it back. Or he could hang it on the bush by the gate. But he pushed it farther down in his pocket and rode back up the street to the old town road.

7

For a week Calder didn't see Mr. Cooley, and she didn't go to the rock. She stayed around Gran's, working in the shop, reading, and wishing something exciting would happen. Today, when she went for the mail, there was a postcard from Dad from Cornwall, England. He wrote: "Of course, I remember that great rock. It's tremendous! I must have taken you up there on my back. But you were probably asleep and not interested in the grandeurs of Nature! Love, Dad."

She wished he were here right this minute. Everything would be exciting if he were here. She folded the card carefully so it would fit into the back pocket of her jeans. There was no sign of Mr. Cooley when she rode slowly past the Inn. She even went up on the porch and looked in the tall jar that held umbrellas and canes beside the front door. Louie wasn't there, either.

Mardie thought it was queer that Mr. Cooley hadn't been down again, especially after he'd been there for dinner. Then she said she wouldn't be at all surprised if he was waiting to come until he could bring the account he was writing of Serpentine Rock. Calder was perfectly sure he wasn't doing that. Mardie hadn't noticed that he didn't ever *say* he'd write one. Neither had Walt made a blazed trail up there.

She had to know whether he had gone for good, so she asked for Mr. Cooley at the desk. He had gone to Boston for ten days but would be back. She felt better, but she rode aimlessly down the street wondering what to do.

"Hi ya," Barbie called out from the front step of the store. She was sitting with Randy and some other boy. "Come on over."

"Hi," Calder answered, wheeling in toward the store, dragging her feet to stop.

"Where ya been?"

"Around." Then she added, "I went climbing."

"You did. Alone?"

"Uhhuh." Calder hesitated, and then said carelessly, "With a boy."

"Who?" Barbie asked; the boys looked interested.

"Walt," she said.

"Walt? Who's he?"

"You mean Walt Bolles, lives up on Old Town Road?" asked the boy she didn't know.

67

"Oh, Calder, this is Bill Yeager."

He and Calder both said, "Hi."

"Sure, I know him. Funny thin guy with kinda long hair; doesn't say much. Hasn't lived here long; he hangs around ball practice sometimes," Bill explained to Randy.

"D'you have fun?" Barbie asked.

"Mhmm." Then pushing down on her pedal, she wheeled off, calling back, "See ya."

"You wanta go swimming?" Barbie called after her. "We're going out. Meet you there."

But by the time Calder had reached Mardie's, her little feeling of triumph had run out. She felt creepy letting Barbie think she had had a date. And what if that Bill said something to Walt about her! He'd hate her more than ever. She certainly wasn't going swimming and have Barbie ask her some more about him.

People were in the shop, of course. They always came down from the Inn after lunch. For something to do, Mardie said, but then they often bought something in spite of themselves, she added.

Calder parked her bike and went down in the back garden. The whole afternoon stretched out in front of her, as empty as the limp hammock under the trees. She went over and lay in the hammock, giving a violent push as she got in. It was fine while the swinging lasted. Above her, she could only see a tiny little piece of sky through the branches of the maple trees. Everywhere she looked there were green maple leaves, layer on layer. That was what was so good about being up on the rock; you could look over the tops of some of the trees, and it made a place in the woods that had nothing but sky above it.

She jumped out of the hammock, and getting her bike, pedalled furiously back up the street toward the Old Town Road. She had to get off and walk at the first steep pitch, but it would be keen coming down. She wondered if the dogs would hear the bicycle before they heard people's feet, but she climbed the wall before they started in. At the beginning of the swamp, she took off her sandals and went barefoot through the cool-feeling mud. She hoped Walt was watching her; she kept an eye on the barn so he couldn't sneak out without her seeing him. She wanted him to come so she could tell him what she thought of him.

That was the tree she had tied her ribbon to, wasn't it? Or was it the one farther over? She wished she had worn a ribbon today so she could tie it on and dare Walt to take it off.

Once over the second wall, the woods blurred into sameness and the barking stopped. No tree stood out as familiar, or maybe they all did. She wasn't high enough up yet. It was queer the way the woods got so still all of a sudden.

If she kept climbing, maybe she could get above the rock and look down on it. She must be over too far. The pine needles stuck to her wet feet. She kept climbing, but no gray shadow appeared. Once she thought she saw the rock, but it was a ledge that came out of the hill, not a round boulder standing alone. The woods darkened as if it were going to rain, so it wasn't easy to see far through the gloomy woods.

If Walt had seen her and was watching her now, the way

he did the other time, he must be laughing at her not being able to find the rock. Where was it? She was looking so hard ahead that she didn't see the branch in front of her that whipped across her face. How could it be harder to find the rock the third time she came up here?

And then it was there, rising up above her through the trees, as sudden as though she had never seen it before. She found the hand hold right away. Climbing with bare feet was lots easier. She didn't need anybody holding his hand for her to step on either. This time, she didn't stand on the rock, but sat in the very center, waiting.

If Walt had sneaked up here and hidden to watch her, he'd have to come out in the open before she made a move. She watched the shadowy woods so hard that she saw a single leaf drift down and light on another before it slid off to the ground. There was a chipmunk! It was getting darker in the woods; a cold breeze made her shiver.

There! The dogs barked. But they stopped too quick for anybody but Walt to be crossing the meadow. He wasn't trying to sneak up on her this time. She heard one stone grate against another on that tumble-down wall, and the sound of his feet as he jumped on the ground. She would just see if *he* could walk right up to the rock. He'd probably made marks on the trees to show him; little marks that nobody else could see.

She must look like a statue, she thought, sitting cross-legged on the top of the rock or like the little Buddha Dad used to have on his bookshelf.

She saw his head—he was coming straight toward the rock. Why didn't he say something? It was eerie waiting.

He was grinning when he came in full sight, but she could tell that he was embarrassed.

She didn't smile back. "At least, you didn't sneak around and hide this time!" she said, before she remembered she was going to wait for him to speak first.

"I only do that when I don't know the people who come up here. Where's the old man?"

"Mr. Cooley is away. I came by myself."

"I saw your bicycle against the wall."

"Of course. *I* wasn't trying to sneak up here."

"Can't anybody with the dogs. Why didn't you go around and keep out of the swamp?"

"I didn't want to," Calder said coolly.

Walt climbed up the pine tree that Calder had climbed and jumped over on the rock to show her it could be done.

"You got your hands covered with pitch," she said.

"That don't matter." He tried to wipe them off on his jeans.

"Where were you?" Calder asked.

"When d'you mean?"

"The time I first found the boulder."

Walt grinned and looked up at her quickly to see if she was mad. "In that beech tree over there. I was right up there where the big branch makes a crook. You coulda seen me if you'd looked hard enough."

Calder studied it. The tree was not very far away.

"I lay so still that I got a crick in my neck. You did look over once when I knocked a piece of bark off. I thought of jumping down and giving a yell, but I was afraid you'd faint." Walt paused. He had never talked so much to a girl

71

he didn't know.

Calder looked disgusted. "I don't faint, silly!"

"But you'd have been scared."

"Maybe," she admitted honestly.

"And you'd have been mad."

"Not any madder than I was when you stood up on the rock and mimicked me."

He reddened and busied himself with digging fallen pine needles out of a deep crack in the rock. If he told her he felt like the King of the Mountain, too, when he stood on top of it, she might not mind so much. Instead he fished in his pocket for the red ribbon and tossed it over to her.

"It's about time," she said. "I wondered if you were going to give it back or keep it." She stuffed it in her pocket.

"Maybe you should tie it back on the tree so you won't have so much trouble finding the boulder next time."

Her eyes flashed. "I found it all right, thank you. Anyway, you said you had to just come on it."

"Look at this," he said abruptly. He was leaning over the side of the rock. "See."

When she knelt beside him, she saw a tiny pink flower growing in a crack—the tiniest little blossom she had ever seen.

"Some bird must've dropped the seed, I figger, and it grew there."

She reached over to pick the flower, and he knocked her hand away. "Leave it be," he said, and then reddened furiously. "You can pick it if you want." She moved back to the center of the rock.

A dull boom of thunder sounded through the woods, seeming to roll down from the hill above them. It left a thick stillness behind. Calder paid no attention.

"Since you can walk straight to the rock, you're never surprised any more, are you?"

Walt looked up quickly. "Oh, yes, I am. That's what's funny about it; the rock's always hidden, an' you always think you'll see it before you do. You keep looking all the time, an' then, there it is."

Thunder rolled again. It would rain in a minute, Calder thought, but she sat as still as though she hadn't heard it.

"Why didn't you bring the old man up here yourself? You didn't even let on you'd been here before, did you?"

Calder shook her head.

"Why didn't you?"

She thought about it, looking off through the gloomy green woods. She didn't know exactly. Under the new grumble of thunder, she said, "It was more secret not telling, I guess."

He knew what she meant. "Haven't you told him yet?"

She shook her head. Lightning cracked a yellow whip across the green woods, bleaching the leaves gray, going into each criss-cross scar on the rock. It made the faces of the two pale and their eyes strangely bright. With a sudden spattering rush, rain poured down on the pine needles and the beech leaves and the surface of the rock. Thunder moved nearer.

"Hey, we're going to get soaked!" Walt said. "Come on."

He didn't have to say where. Calder slid down over the

73

side of the rock and ran to the overhanging bulge of the boulder, just as the yellow whip cracked again. Walt came after her, flattening himself against the rock. Neither of them spoke. The rain poured down a curtain that shut them into a shallow cave. Calder pushed so close against the rock that she could feel the hard ridges against her back.

"You're too far over, you're getting all wet. Move in more," she said.

"It won't last," he said, edging a couple of inches nearer. "It don't when it comes down in buckets all of a sudden like that."

"I don't mind the rain. I wish the lightning would stop. Can you get struck if you're under a rock?"

"Naw. We're safe as anything under here," Walt said, but he wasn't sure.

The thunder boomed on the rock above their heads, and the lightning slashed a furrow of lemon yellow on the ground so near that Calder drew her feet in under her. "Maybe we should run for it."

"Then the lightning *could* get us. It oughta slack up pretty soon."

They waited silently. Calder wished she were home. Walt knew his aunt would ask him why he didn't have enough sense to come in out of the rain and where was he, anyway?

Lightning snapped close to them, followed by the splitting sound of wood, then a crash. Walt ducked out to look, standing with the rain coming down on him.

"Golly Moses! It struck right down the center of the tree over there! It coulda set it on fire, but I guess the tree was too wet."

74

Calder shivered. Her face had turned a yellowish white.

"You cold?" Walt asked.

"Not much, but it's about as cold as winter."

"Maybe the ice age is coming back!" Walt managed to grin, pushing his wet hair out of his eyes. "Wouldn't that be something! A sheet of ice coming down over the whole earth! Maybe it'll take Serpentine with it again and roll it two hunderd more miles."

"And when it hits the wall down there, it'll send all the stones rolling like bowling pins," Calder went on.

"Not in front of it; underneath. The ice comes in a sheet and covers everything."

Unimpressed, Calder said, "It would have to be some force to move this rock."

"Are you kidding! This rock would be nothing but a pebble to a glacier. The glacier'd start up in the Arctic somewheres, an' by the time it got here, it would move faster an' faster. You should see what it's like here in winter!"

She tried to think how it would be. "I'd sure like to be here in winter—just to see everything. Is the rock all covered by snow?"

"I didn't come to the farm till February, but you shoulda seen the snow four feet thick on the barn roof, an' icicles as tall as I am hanging from the roof of the house. I had to go out every morning and whack 'em down an' jump outa the way, 'cause they'd go right through you an' you'd be dead. I had to hang outa the upstairs winder to get some of them. I didn't find the rock right away. The snow was over part of it, so it looked like part of a cliff. It's sorta nice in here in the woods some days in March, except the snow drifts are so deep.'' He stopped, embarrassed at talking so much.

''When did you really see what it was?''

''Not till late April. After a rain had washed the snow off. I couldn't believe the way it was—was just here. And so big!''

''I couldn't when I saw it, either.''

They were two explorers, comparing their discoveries.

''There was plenty of snow still around it, but where the sun got to it, you could see how round it was. What'd he call it?''

''An erratic boulder, because it—''

''I know why,'' Walt interrupted. ''I just forgot the word.''

The thunder was drawing back from the valley. The rain had lost its force; lightning flashed weakly.

''Let's go see the tree that got struck,'' Walt said.

The split-off limb made an awkward angle with the trunk; one great bough spread out on the ground. Calder walked up the wet limb, teetering a little to keep her balance. Jagged spikes of wood stuck up from the split. Walt came just behind her.

''When you look at the way it broke off, it's no wonder it made such an awful sound.''

''It was the worst, most agonizing sound I ever heard. The tree didn't want to be wrenched apart like that, and it was crying out,'' Calder said.

Walt looked at her solemn face as she stood above him on the limb of the tree. She said the queerest things, but he guessed it had sounded a little like that. He didn't know what to say so he jumped to the ground. Calder walked back down in her bare feet, dainty like. Her hair was so wet it looked dark instead of light. She was soaked all over.

"You want to come up to the house and get a sweater or something?" he asked, wondering uneasily what Aunt Lil would say.

"No. It won't take me long to get home. Gran'll be making a great rumpus about not knowing where I am in the storm, as it is. Beat you to the wall," she said, running headlong down through the woods, but she slipped, and stood stork-legged, putting on her sandals.

Like a girl, he thought, as he stood by the wall waiting for her. Didn't admit he'd beat. The minute they climbed the wall, the barking began.

"How do the dogs know when we're still way up here?"

"Search me. But they do. Shut up!" he yelled out across the meadow. The barking decreased a little. "You hear me, shut up!" he shouted again. The barking thinned to an occasional yelp.

"How can you bear to keep them locked up in that old barn?"

"They don't know any differ'nt."

"They know the difference between being in prison and being free. I'd be ashamed to do that to an animal."

"They got a pen out back of the barn they go to sometimes. Anyway, it isn't my doing; they belong to Aunt Lil," he muttered crossly. It was none of her business.

"The mud's ice cold," Calder said, as they started across the meadow. When they came to the wall that bordered the road, Walt blurted out quickly, "You aren't still mad, are you? About my spying on you an' yelling from the rock?"

Calder stood still, considering. "I guess not. It's your rock, only you didn't have to make fun of me!"

She picked up her bike and wheeled off without looking back.

"Watch out on the hill. The road'll be slippery," he called after her.

Calder kept going at top speed.

8

"Picnic weather, absolutely! Did you ever see a lovelier day, Calder?" Mardie was already sitting at breakfast on the porch when Calder came out. "That's why we absolutely had to have strawberries on our cereal."

Calder was used now to jumping with Mardie's sentences. She crushed a plump berry against the roof of her mouth with her tongue rather than biting into it. The berry was so ripe that a little juice ran out between her lips.

"Calder! What on earth are you doing?"

Calder swallowed hurriedly and licked her lips. "You taste the berry more if you squash it instead of biting into it. Dad and I made an experiment."

Mardie frowned. She had put Jean's first husband out of

79

her mind as an unpleasant quantity, and she didn't like having Calder bring him so constantly before her. "Well, it looks perfectly awful. Don't ever do such a thing again at the table."

But Calder could tell that Mardie wasn't really cross. She went right back to the day. "Sometimes, I think it takes the severe winters up here to produce such glorious summer days. You don't get days like this in California!"

Calder's mouth was too full to answer.

"I do hope your mother will get back here this summer."

Calder put her glass of milk down quickly. "Did she say she might?"

"Oh, no. I'm just always hoping she'll get back each summer."

"If she came, we could go back together," Calder said. "That would be fun."

Mardie went on. "It's so absolutely beautiful, I thought when I woke up, this is the day to take a picnic to Serpentine Rock. Mr. Cooley is back, and I promised him we'd make an expedition, you know."

"He's already been there," Calder said. "Maybe he won't want to go again."

"Of course, he will to a picnic. And I thought I'd get that Bolles boy to go with us. That would be a treat for him, and there are things I want him to do."

Calder wondered what Walt would think if Gran went up there.

"Dear, you ride up to the Inn and ask Mr. Cooley if he would like to go. Tell him I'll drive up to the Inn about eleven and pick him up."

Mardie was like Mother the way she decided things so fast.

"I have the most perfect picnic hamper that we bought in England." Mardie was on her way to the kitchen, and her voice trailed behind her. "Do you want lemonade or milk on the picnic, Calder?"

"I don't care," Calder said. She wondered if there was a chance that Mother might come. She would write her tonight.

Mr. Cooley was on his way up the street as Calder came along, and he waved Louie at her. "I'm glad to see you, Calder. When I stopped in at the shop to see your grandmother, you weren't there. It rained so hard that I stayed for tea, but still you didn't come!"

"I was up at the boulder. I got soaked. Oh, Mr. Cooley, Gran wants to take a picnic up to the rock. She's already putting up the lunch. And she's coming up in the jeep to pick you up at eleven." Calder's words fell over each other. "She wants Walt to go with us, and I don't think he'll like it. I guess we have to go, though. You will come, won't you?"

Mr. Cooley laughed. "I wouldn't miss such an expedition for anything. Louie and I will be waiting on the porch. Shall I assure her that we could take her there without bothering Walt?"

"No, because I think she wants him on account of getting him to make a trail."

"Ah, of course! And she wants me to go so she can spur me on to write that account of the rock for her circular." He tipped his head to one side, with one eyebrow raised. "Mrs. Calder has no idea how long it takes me to put pen to paper."

When Calder got back, Mardie was dressed for the picnic in blue slacks and sweater and a ribbon around her head like a girl. Calder looked at her and looked quickly away. Gran's red tennis shoes didn't have a spot on them, so they'd have to go around that other way.

"Just put the hamper in the jeep, dear. I had this in mind yesterday, so I had fried chicken and cookies ready in case the weather was good. And I have a surprise for everyone." She put a flat package on the floor of the car, along with a kind of knitting bag and a blanket.

"This is quite an expedition," Mr. Cooley said, as he got in front with Gran.

The road seemed different going over it so fast without stopping to rest. Mardie drove right into the yard of the Bolles' farm and parked in front of the back porch. When she turned off the ignition, the dogs' barking filled the summer morning.

"Gracious! Where are those dogs?"

"Oh, they're shut up in the barn, Gran. They can't get out."

"I should hope they couldn't. They're enough to scare the life out of you."

A thin, sandy-haired woman opened the screen door. She wore pants, too; old blue jeans and a man's shirt, with the sleeves rolled above her elbows. Her hair was cut short and fell straight. She didn't look the least bit like Walt, Calder

thought to herself.

"Good morning, Mrs. Bolles. You remember me, I'm Martha Calder." The tone of Gran's voice was like maple syrup. It made Calder squirm. "Isn't this a beautiful day!"

"It's going to be hot before it's done," Mrs. Bolles answered.

"We're planning a picnic, and we would like to have it up at Serpentine Rock, if that's all right with you. And we'd like to have your nephew go with us. May we interrupt his work that long?"

"Sure, you can go. Plenty of folks do without asking, and I can't stop 'em. As to Walt; you'll have to ask him. He's weeding down back of the house."

"Calder—this is my granddaughter, Mrs. Bolles."

Calder said how do you do quickly. She wanted to warn Walt.

"Calder, you can go and invite him to join us. My, you can hardly hear yourself think with those dogs barking. How do you put up with it? it?" Mardie asked.

"They're good watch dogs," Mrs. Bolles told her, but she was looking at Calder, who disappeared around the house.

"Can you stop them barking if you speak to them?"

"No. They don't do any harm, and then I know if anybody's on the place. You get used to them."

"This is Mr. Cooley, Mrs. Bolles. Mr. Cooley is a geologist and very much interested in the rock."

Mrs. Bolles nodded. "Pleased to meet you," she said in answer to Mr. Cooley's greeting. "Lots of people have been interested in the rock."

"You know, I haven't been up to Serpentine in years," Mardie told Mrs. Bolles. "And now that the trees have grown up so, I don't believe I could find it. It seems such a pity when it's one of the chief points of interest in the town, and visitors would like to see it."

"I don't care much for folks traipsing over the pasture and laying down the barbed wire and all. They do enough damage during hunting season."

"Oh, but that's just the point. They wouldn't if there were a trail, and the trees were cut down around the rock."

Mrs. Bolles made no reply, but her eyes moved across the road, up the hill, in the direction of the rock.

"If it were cleared out, you could see the rock right from your porch," Mardie went on. "I should think that the

Town Development Society could pay you for the trees that would need to be taken down. There wouldn't have to be too many, but enough so that people could see the rock from the road the way they used to be able to do. You remember the postcard."

"No, I can't say I do, but I remember the rock when it was all bare up there. Folks went up to the rock more than they do now, and kids left their picnic trash around."

Mr. Cooley and Louie moved a little distance away from the discussion, until Calder came back with Walt.

"How do you do, young man," Mardie said. "How would you like to join us in a picnic at the rock?"

Walt looked uneasily from Mardie to his aunt. He gave a half smile. "Sure, I guess so. I haven't fixed any trail yet."

"Perhaps it's just as well. We can plan it as we go." Mardie turned back to Mrs. Bolles. "I spoke to your nephew in town one day about blazing a trail and clearing a little path to the rock. I'm president of the Weldon Development Society."

"He didn't say anything about it to me," Mrs. Bolles said.

"You wouldn't have any objection, would you?"

Something seemed to happen in Mrs. Bolles' face, Calder thought. It looked sort of closed at first, as though she was going to say she would mind. Then she looked off toward the hill, and said, "No it won't affect me any." Calder was disappointed. "Walt, if you're going on a picnic you better go change that shirt and wash up." Walt reddened, as he disappeared inside the kitchen door.

"Mrs. Bolles, wouldn't you like to come with us?"

Mardie offered suddenly. "We have oceans of food."

"No, thank you. I'm not much on picnics," Mrs. Bolles said. "And I got plenty to do right here."

Calder went over to Mr. Cooley. "Walt didn't want to go," she said in a low voice. "But I told him he had to."

Mr. Cooley smiled. "You should have told him that the League for the Prevention of Publicizing the Erratic Boulder must hang together."

Mr. Cooley was wonderful. They would be a club and band together against Gran and the Development Society.

"Well, we're sorry you won't join us, Mrs. Bolles," Gran said, as Walt came back in clean shirt and jeans, his hair slicked down with water, all but the cluster of hairs that stood up out of the crown of his head. "Now where, Walter?"

"Maybe you better drive down the old road by the cemetery, 'cause our meadow is all swamp."

They piled back into the jeep, Mr. Cooley beside Gran, and Walt and Calder in back.

"Mr. Cooley says we'll have to form a League for the Prevention of Publicizing the Erratic Boulder," Calder told Walt.

"The what?" Walt asked, but Mardie turned her head to ask, "How far do we go? This old road looks so overgrown."

"It's O.K. It's a good solid road. You can stop right by the cemetery gates," Walt directed.

The jeep eased itself like an old man down the steep pitch to a little bridge, wheezed up the other side, and stopped with a relieved puff of exhausted breath.

"Isn't this the most peaceful spot, Mr. Cooley!" Mardie exclaimed. "Some of those are Revolutionary soldiers' graves."

"I like the way the pines and balsams guard the cemetery," Mr. Cooley said.

"Yes, and just smell them!"

"You know, there was an old legend that when the graves of saints were opened, a fragrance of balsam rose from them," Mr. Cooley told them. "Here, the balsam and pine smell makes all these graves those of saints!"

"Why what a perfectly darling idea! But I doubt very much if they were all saints!" Her laughter floated over Walt and Calder without touching them. Calder was staring at the gravestones, many of them tipped. She wished the graves could open and the people under the grass could step out. Maybe all the winters and springs and falls and summers *had* made them into saints. And the children would be little saints.

"Walter, you may carry the hamper, and Mr. Cooley, if you'll please take the blanket. Calder, here are some strips of red cloth I tore apart. We'll tie them on the trees that Walter is going to blaze later. And you can carry the extra Thermos case."

"We might as well climb over the wall here," Walt said.

"Now, wait, I think we'd better make an opening in the wall, so people won't have to climb over it, and then they'll see where to go."

"But is that quite legal, Mrs. Calder?" Mr. Cooley asked. "Isn't it a law of the land that you don't knock down a man's wall?"

"But this is an old tumble-down wall, and there aren't any animals in the field. I'm sure we could make just a narrow opening—say, two stones' width—without bothering anyone."

Walt and Calder and Mr. Cooley stood looking at the wall without offering to move any stones. "It's easy enough to step over," Mr. Cooley said.

"Walter, is this your aunt's wall?"

"Yes, it is, and my father's. They both own this land," he said proudly.

"Well, would they mind if we just made a small opening here?"

Walt shifted the hamper from one hand to the other. It wasn't light. He could feel Calder looking at him. "I don't think they'd like it much," he said.

"My word!" Mardie exclaimed. "Very well, we'll have to move farther along here where there's a tree." They moved together up the faint ruts of the old road. Mardie stopped when they came to a white birch growing close to the wall. "I like this better, anyway! And it will add to the adventure to have people have to climb over the wall. Now!" She laid her bag on the ground and began unwrapping her package.

"This is my surprise, for I'm sure you didn't think I'd have it ready!" She held up a rustic sign made of a pine board, with the words "TO SERPENTINE ROCK" burned into the wood and an arrow pointing. "Isn't it nicely done!" Her three companions stared at it.

"You suit the action to the word," Mr. Cooley murmured. Walt and Calder were silent.

Mardie was rummaging in her bag and brought out a hammer and a little jar of nails. "Just set down that hamper, Walter, and nail this sign on the tree. Then I thought, if they were close enough together, we'd only have blazes on the trees the rest of the way and clear a path, of course. I brought some fine brush clippers along."

"Gran, you don't want to put up a sign like that!" Calder burst out.

"You aren't supposed to do anything to hurt white birch trees," Walt said.

"Like stripping off the bark; I wouldn't think of doing that. But two nails aren't going to hurt the tree." Mardie held the sign up against the main crotch in the tree. "About there, wouldn't you think, Mr. Cooley?"

The sun caught the newly varnished surface of the board and made the burned letters stand out.

"I'm sure that Walt is correct about harming birch trees, and there may be a law against pounding a nail in one," Mr. Cooley observed mildly.

Mardie's irritation showed in the way her mouth moved. "I think that's straining at a gnat! Besides, this tree would be on your aunt's property, Walter, and she said she wouldn't mind our cutting down a few trees." She selected a nail from the jar.

Mr. Cooley came over to her. "Well, if Walt thinks it will be all right," he said, taking the sign from Mardie.

Walt looked at Calder. "I oughta ask my father first," he said.

Mardie ignored his remark. "I believe it ought to be a little lower. It really is a handsome sign. Right there, Mr.

Cooley; and see that the arrow points straight up toward the woods."

The sound of the hammer blows echoed through the valley and started the dogs barking again, but they sounded farther away here.

"There! That's very attractive with the pine against the birch and the leaves hanging down that way." Mardie stood off to admire it.

"It looks like a public park sign," Calder muttered.

"I never heard anything more ridiculous, Calder. You can't possibly make a Vermont hillside look like a public park by simply putting up an attractive rustic sign. Now, all three of you stand in front of it, and I'll take a picture." She brought her camera out of her bag. "You'll have to stand closer together. Walter, you and Calder kneel down, and Mr. Cooley, stand behind them. Smile a little, Calder." They stood fixed until the click of the camera released them.

Calder absolutely abominated the way Mardie bossed everyone, as though this were her hill and her rock. They spread out across the open field, Walt a little ahead. No one spoke for a few minutes.

"My, it is good to get out on these hills! I should do it more often," Mardie said to Mr. Cooley.

Calder wondered gloomily if Gran would want to go to the rock all the time now. The field had grown up to blackberry bushes that caught on the blanket Mr. Cooley carried, so he stopped to roll it tighter and carry it on his shoulder. Why would Gran need to bring a blanket along, anyway?

"We must clear out these blackberry bushes, Walter, but

91

I suppose you can do it later," Mardie said. "And we need to make sure that anyone starting across this field will see the next blaze. Perhaps we should put up a stake about here, and maybe you could burn an arrow into a little piece of wood, Calder."

The rest of the company surveyed the spot without comment, until Mr. Cooley said, "I would think anyone who wanted to see the rock would have enough perseverance to cross the field, at least, and keep in the direction of the arrow on the big sign. You don't want to take away all sense of a quest."

Calder rolled the word *quest* over in her mind. It was in the *Idylls of the King,* in the last book, where they all went off on a quest for the Holy Grail, and King Arthur didn't like their leaving the court and all they ought to be doing there. The thought pleased her. Finding the rock *had* been a quest. But it would be spoiled when Gran got through with it. Grasshoppers zinged in the field. The hot sun drew up the smell of grass and red clover. If only she and Walt and Mr. Cooley were by themselves, it would be lovely.

Walt turned up toward the stone wall.

"Right here, Calder. Tie one of your pieces of cloth to this tree . . ."

Calder pulled a string of red cloth from her pocket and tied it to a twig, without looking at Walt who stood waiting.

"If you had a red hair ribbon, you could use that," he said.

Mardie glanced at him. The remark hardly seemed to make sense to her, but Mr. Cooley laughed.

"I might not get it back," Calder said, and then in a

92

lower voice, she added, "I wouldn't be surprised if this one disappears."

"Good gracious, these woods have grown up! You couldn't possibly find the rock, if you didn't know where it was," Mardie said.

"If it was a quest, you could," Calder said.

"Of course, I suppose you could, if you combed the whole hill. But how many visitors to the town want to do that? How did you find it, Walter? Of course, your aunt could tell you about where it is."

"Oh, I just stumbled on it. Aunt Lil didn't ever say anything about it, so I wasn't looking for it."

"It's farther than I remembered, and harder climbing," Mardie said. "I'm glad I didn't bring Viva along. Now, Calder, I think another marker about here." Calder's eyes met Mr. Cooley's. He raised one eyebrow that funny way he did.

"This is a much longer way," Mr. Cooley said, coming up beside Calder. "It's hard to tell whether we're up high enough."

"I think I'll rest a minute," Gran said, and Mr. Cooley waited with her. Calder caught up with Walt.

"What are you going to do about the blazes?" Calder asked.

"Oh, I won't make 'em very deep. They'll grow over quick."

"You know this was all Gran's idea," Calder said anxiously.

"Sure, I know. She's like Aunt Lil. If she gets an idea to have you do something, she keeps harping on it till you do it." They could see Mardie and Mr. Cooley coming now.

"How far would you say it is?" Mardie asked. "You know, it might be a good idea to put the distance on the big sign."

"About a half mile," Mr. Cooley said. "I should have worn my pedometer." Just then he saw the rock far ahead, blocking the space between the trees. There was something strange about it. He had seen larger erratic boulders than this before, but he had never had one strike him as having a ghostly presence. Perhaps he was seeing it through the children's eyes. He looked at Calder and Walt. They were ahead, close to the rock, but if they saw it, they gave no sign.

"I had no idea the trees were so big in here. Look at that beech tree ahead," Mardie was saying. She had looked right past the rock. "Of course, thirty years or so is a long time. I'm coming. Don't wait for me," she called out, seeing them just standing there. "I'm really enjoying the hike." But they went on standing. She came up to them; then she saw the rock.

"Why, there it is! It seems so shrunken in size, crowded in like this. You can't get far enough from it to see its size, can you? We must have all these trees cut down so there's a real space around it, particularly on this side, as you approach it. Because, really, it's a very big rock. How big would you say, Mr. Cooley? You must get that in your article." She went over to the picnic hamper.

Gran wasn't the least little bit impressed. Calder laid her hand on the rock, apologizing to it in a way.

"Calder, if you and Walter will spread out the blanket

94

right here, we can spread the tablecloth."

Calder picked up the blanket and shook it out on the ground without waiting for Walt to help. "The ground slopes too much here, Mardie. We better go over there."

"We really ought to eat on top of the rock," Mr. Cooley suggested.

"I've done it," Mardie said. "Time was when I used to climb it and think nothing of it. We must have a rustic ladder built, so young people can get up easily. We always had one here."

Calder's eyes met Walt's and slid over to meet Mr. Cooley's glance.

"We'll just have a buffet!" Mardie said. "Here are cups, Calder. There is coffee and lemonade."

The lunch did look good. Fried chicken and deviled eggs, and three kinds of little sandwiches, and cookies, and oranges. Everyone's paper plate was loaded. Calder sat down on the ground with her back to the rock. She didn't want to look at it. Mardie sat on a lower part of the ledge by the picnic. Mr. Cooley and Walt found places facing the rock.

"This is a banquet instead of a picnic," Mr. Cooley said. Walt was eating so steadily that he had no time for conversation. Calder was eating, too, but she was thinking that the rock would never be the same to her.

"When we used to picnic up here, we always came for supper because it was too hot right out in the open without a bit of shade around it. Now there are so many trees in here, it's almost sombre."

Calder finished a drumstick. "The rock makes the place

solemn more than the trees do.''

"Yes," Mardie agreed. "Crowded in this way by the trees, it's a little overpowering. But when we get some of the closest trees cut down, it will be much better. Whom do you think we could get to cut down these trees, Walter?"

"I don't know. I'll be going to see my dad sometime this month. I'll ask him whether it's all right with him."

"Of course, we'll have the wood cut up and stacked at your house so your aunt can burn it," Mardie went on.

"We have an electric stove," Walt said. "And there isn't any fireplace."

"Will you have another cup of coffee, Mr. Cooley?"

Walt wouldn't know, but Mardie used that tone of voice after you'd been rude; terribly polite and sweet to show how you *should* sound.

Mardie had begun to pick up the food. "Here's a special container for the used plates and napkins and debris. Wouldn't it be fine if there were a stone fireplace up here!"

"Gollee! Are you goin' to have a table an' benches an' a can with 'Keep Vermont Beautiful' on it?" Walt burst out.

Mardie laughed gaily. "You never can tell, but not right away. That would cost more than the Development Society would want to raise. Folders with the story of the rock are more important first. How are you coming with your account of it, Mr. Cooley?"

Mr. Cooley shook his head. "I'm ashamed to admit that I'm very slow about these things, Mrs. Calder. I had to go to Boston, and I really haven't had time to get at it."

In the silence Calder could feel Mardie's disappointment with him. But he was filling his pipe and didn't seem to notice. "Aren't you going to climb up on the rock before we go?" he said to Walt and Calder.

But when she was up on the rock, with all of them standing down there and the picnic things on the yellow cloth, Calder felt it was different from any other time. "Come on," she said to Walt. He climbed up, but then they just stood there. "It spoils everything," Calder muttered to him. Walt nodded.

"Let me give you a hand to stand on, Mrs. Calder, and you can take hold of Walt's," Mr. Cooley said.

"Oh, I haven't been up on the rock for so many years, I—Well, all right." Mardie stepped on Mr. Cooley's hand and Walt and Calder both pulled her from the top. "That's not bad for an old lady like me," Mardie said with a pleased little laugh. "But there's no view at all, anymore! You used to be able to see way down the valley to the village. Really, it's a crime these trees have been allowed to grow like this. What was your uncle thinking of, Walter? Why didn't he have some animals grazing here, at least?"

"I don't know," Walt said sulkily.

"Mr. Cooley said it was the wilderness taking back its own," Calder said. "I like it this way."

Mr. Cooley was climbing up, too; and then they all stood there like the Pilgrims landing on Plymouth Rock, Calder thought.

"There used to be a smaller rock perched on top, like a rocking chair," Mardie said. "Anyone who sat on it and rocked was very daring."

"Did you?" Calder asked.

"Yes, indeed, when I was your age. I never thought then

97

that I'd ever climb up here in my sixties. I guess I never thought of being that old.'' She gave a funny little laugh that made Calder uncomfortable. It was horrid with them all standing up on the rock. With everyone there, the rock that she had found by herself was just a big old rock with nothing secret about it at all. Calder slid down the side, wanting to leave.

"I guess we better start back," Mardie said. Mr. Cooley let himself down first. Mardie hesitated. "It looks harder to get down."

"Just turn around and let yourself slide against the rock," Mr. Cooley directed. Walt took hold of her hand. Mr. Cooley helped her so she slid down slowly.

Calder picked up the blanket and Thermos case and started on ahead of the others. She was having what Dad would call one of her silent times when she didn't feel like talking. The rock was as good as lost. It didn't seem erratic or mysterious. It was even hard to remember how it had come through all that long journey, and been knocked around, and grated against other rocks, and carried by that ice sheet ages and ages ago. It was just ordinary; a place for people to go for a picnic. She felt as if she had lost her watch or a library book that would take her next ten allowances to pay for.

"Calder! Calder, dear, wait for us! I want you to tie another marker just about where you are standing," Mardie called.

Calder turned. Back of them, she could still make out the rock, but it seemed already to be drawing away behind the trees into its own safe place.

"O.K., Gran," she called back. "Here?" As Walt came up to her, she murmured, "Be sure you take them all off by tomorrow, for sure."

"Don't worry!" he promised.

9

The day Aunt Lil was gone until evening, Walt worked faithfully all morning. He wondered where she'd gone, but she just said she had to go on business in Rutland. Having the place to himself was nice. He let the dogs out, because he hadn't liked that girl's saying it was like keeping the dogs in prison to keep them shut up. They blinked at all the light, and Fido lifted his head to smell, as though the air outside the barn was different or that there was so much of it, maybe. If a prisoner were hidden inside of Brownie's skin, he'd be a fat nice sort of man, Walt thought. Fido took off down the road, and Walt had to yell himself hoarse before he came back. Both of them acted half crazy. When Walt took them down to the garden with him, they trampled over everything and he had to get out of the garden himself to get them out. It wasn't easy to drag 'em back into the barn, but he finally got them shut in. He wondered if Aunt Lil had ever let 'em out by herself. Maybe this afternoon he'd take 'em for a run; maybe he'd take 'em to the rock.

At noon, he came back up to the house and ate the cold beans and brown bread and rhubarb pie and milk that Aunt Lil had left out in the pantry, but he took the food out on the porch and ate, the way they were doing at that girl's house that night. It was nice with the sun coming across the table and the dogs quiet. There was a swell view from the porch. He thought of his father being a boy here and wondered about his never really coming back here to live, once he'd graduated from high school. After he got out of the Vet'rans' Hospital, his father would come back and stay here till he got strong. Walt took his dishes in and washed them and put them away, even though there were only two plates and his glass and a fork. Aunt Lil was always telling him men and boys oughta be as neat and handy as women, and there wasn't any reason why they had to be waited on and taken care of. Taken care of and waited on seemed like two differ'nt things, when you thought about it.

By mid-afternoon, he'd done everything he could think of to do; even burned the trash, and Aunt Lil hadn't told him to do that. He stood right by it till the fire was all out. Then he decided to go up to the rock.

It was differ'nt from the way it was last spring when he'd just found it. It didn't seem so much his. That girl had made it part hers, talking about it being a castle, and finding it by herself that way. She'd kept secret about finding it, though,

101

and she hadn't stayed mad about his making fun of her. Maybe she'd come up today. He never called her by her name to himself; just "she" or "that girl."

He let the dogs out, and they almost knocked him down bursting out of the dark barn. They barked and went in circles, and he had to yell at them ten times to get them started across the meadow. The swamp slowed 'em down some. Fido lay right down in the mud. He guessed it felt good and cool. Brownie kept jumping, he was so short legged. If the girl came today, she'd like the dogs being out. She'd see that all the red rags were gone, too.

Once over the wall, the dogs kept picking up smells and running all over the hill. Brownie gave quick, high little yelps like he'd found something. The whole valley echoed. It was good there wasn't anyone close enough to wonder what was up.

Walt knew the shape of the stone on the wall where he always climbed over into the wood and the shape of the spindly maple just beyond it, and then the big pine, and the outcropping of rock—it was as good as a trail. But still he kept his eyes ahead, looking hard through the trees to catch the first glimpse.

There! Right on the nose! He hadn't wasted a step going to it. The rock seemed like his every time when he first saw it. He was always half afraid it wouldn't seem as big as the last time, but it did—and solid. Of course, a rock would be solid, only this was differ'nt— He didn't know what he meant exactly. Maybe that girl would.

The dogs came pell-mell through the woods. Fido tried to jump over a fallen limb and got tangled up in the branches.

Brownie just squirmed underneath. Fido set up such a fuss that he went over and grabbed him by the collar to get him free. But when he climbed up on the rock, the dogs went frantic again, wanting to get up there. If they were mad dogs, or blood-thirsty ones, they could keep a man up on the rock till he starved to death. He wished she would come and they could play they were held here. She was always making up things; that was kid stuff for him.

"Shut up!" he yelled at them, and stretched out flat on the rock in spite of their barking. The sun came down through the pine branches, warm and medicine-smelling. He reached his arms out on the rock, rubbing the back of the hand that had the mosquito-bite on it against the rough surface. Then he just lay quiet, looking up at the clear piece of sky over him, watching the little clouds, until he felt as if the rock were loosening from the earth, moving ever so little. It didn't worry him that he'd be underneath if it rolled; or no, he supposed he'd be thrown off, and the rock would come over him, flattening him into the ground. He'd like to tell her how it felt. Try it, if you don't believe you feel you're moving. If you think you can lie still that long, he'd say. You have to lie as still as though you're dead and keep your eyes on the clouds. She never stayed still for more than a moment. Anyway, he'd told her enough. She hadn't thought it was anything when he told her about whacking down the icicles.

The dogs had given up trying to jump on the rock. They lay on the ground, panting. The sound was loud; everything else was so quiet. Like somebody breathing close to you in the woods, somebody creeping up on you. He sat up

103

suddenly, and the dogs were up. Fido whined. Brownie let out high quick yelps.

"O.K., dogs, I'm coming." He wanted to get them back before Aunt Lil came. She'd said they were always to stay in the barn. He ran, watching them plunge and wallow through the swampy places. But when he got to the barn, they wouldn't go in. He went in and whistled and called, but they stayed outside. He hustled to pour dog chow in their pans and stood in the doorway rattling the tin dishes together. They came then, but just as they got to the door they were off again.

"See if I ever let you out again!" he stormed, and then changed his voice to a pleading tone. "Come on, pups. Here, Fido, here Brownie, there's a good dog!"

He saw Aunt Lil's old car coming up the road before the dogs did, but the next second, they were after it, barking at the top of their voices, going so close to the car that Walt was afraid they'd be run over. Aunt Lil would be mad. She kept coming right toward the dogs till she got to the barn. When she opened the door, Fido hurled himself at her. Walt grabbed his collar, pulling him over backward, but falling under him on the ground. He hung on, trying to roll out from under. He felt the dog's teeth on his arm.

"Let him go, Walt!" his aunt yelled, kicking out at the dog. Walt let go, and ran for the barn with Fido after him. Walt ran up the stairs to the loft just as Fido caught the bottom of his jeans. The old cloth tore off in his teeth, and Walt got a board across the stairs.

Aunt Lil banged the barn doors closed on the dogs. "You climb out onto the roof of the calf shed," she called to him.

Walt hated to go up to the house and face her, but there was nothing else for it. He opened the screen door.

"Well, I guess you've learned your lesson," Aunt Lil said. "Next time, maybe you'll do what you're told. Let's see your arm. At least, the dog wasn't mad; he had his rabies shot when the vet tested the cow."

"Gee, Aunt Lil, I just wanted to give 'em a run once up on the hill."

She was busy getting out iodine and tearing a sheet for a bandage. The iodine burned like fire. He sucked in his breath and bit his lips to keep from yelling.

"I know it hurts," Aunt Lil said. There was something in her voice he'd never heard before that kinda helped the burning. "I might have been putting this on my own leg if you hadn't grabbed him," she said.

"I never thought Fido would really bite."

"Those dogs were brought up to be watch dogs. That's why we never treated them like house pets. I was glad to have them here, when I was alone. If that don't look good tomorrow, we'll get you to town to the doctor, but I think it'll be all right."

Aunt Lil wouldn't let him dry the dishes. "Nope. We'll let the dishes dry themselves. I want to talk to you, Walt."

Now it was coming. He thought she'd been awful easy on him for disobeying. He didn't like a woman scolding him. His father'd always told him off at home. Walt fixed his eyes on the calendar on the wall.

"I went to see your father today," Aunt Lil said.

Color rushed into his face. Why couldn't she have let him go, too?

106

As though she knew what he was thinking, she said, "I didn't take you along because I wanted to talk business, but I'll be going back again soon, and then you can go."

"How is he?"

"Not very good, Walt. He's going to have to stay there a long time. I went to see him about selling the farm." She was tracing the pattern on the red oilcloth, and Walt watched her finger instead of looking at her face.

"It's pretty hard for me living off up here in winter. A man made a good offer for the place a couple of weeks ago, and it seems as though we oughta snap it up."

Walt's eyes flew to her face.

"I'll move to Spencer where I can get something to do, and you'll be close to school. It'll be a lot better for you. Your father thinks so, too. Next week, I'll take the papers in for your father to sign."

When Walt didn't say anything, she asked, "You'd like being in town again, wouldn't you?"

He hadn't got to thinking about that yet. He noticed how the first day in the month was a blank space on the calendar. "I like it here all right," he said.

"You've been a big help; I told your father so. And company," Aunt Lil said. He hadn't known before whether she liked having him here or not.

"Will you sell the woodlot with the rock on it, too?"

"Yes," his aunt said. "I don't suppose the man knows about the rock, but he's interested in the timber on the place."

"Does Dad really want you to sell it?"

"I guess, Walt, it isn't a question of what he wants. It's a question of what is best—for you as much as anyone. Your father's got plans for you, you know. He wants you should go on to college when you finish high school, for one thing. That takes a lot of money.''

''Don't let's sell this place, Aunt Lil. I'll work twice as hard. I want to talk to Dad about it first.'' He was afraid he was going to blubber in a minute, right in front of her, so he turned his face away.

Aunt Lil shook her head. ''It was hard enough for your father to make up his mind to sell without making him go all over it again. I've seen too many people who've hung onto old farms because they didn't want to give 'em up, and the farms have got on top of 'em, just like the dog got on top of you. This farm was on your uncle's back for years. We only just got by. Your father knows that. If he was so fond of it, he could have come back here now and then.''

Walt hardly listened to what she was saying. His arm ached, and his dad was going to have to stay in that place for a long time; that meant all the rest of the summer and next winter. He moved across the kitchen and opened the door to the stairs.

''I guess I'll go to bed now,'' he said.

In his own room, he sprawled on the bed without undressing, and pulled the pillow over his head.

10

Calder had got in the habit of going over to the Inn to see Mr. Cooley every morning when she went for the mail. He was usually on the porch, reading the paper, Louie propped against the chair beside him.

This morning, he looked up with a smile and held up a pad of ruled paper. "I thought I ought to make a start on this story about the rock before I go down to see your Grandmother again."

"I thought you weren't going to write it. The minute you get it done, Gran'll have it printed." Calder looked so alarmed, he laughed.

"I'm sure she will, but I said 'a start.' I told her I wrote very slowly. But it's been a week since we went on our

109

picnic, and I can't say that other pressing business claims my attention exactly.''

Calder considered. "Can't you be working on something else first? Dad always says he has several irons in the fire when people ask him if he's working on a new novel.''

"As a matter of fact, I am, but I can't put her off forever. Oh, don't worry, Calder, this will be very dull and need several revisions and consultations. Perhaps, I shall even need to consult sources. You see how far I've come.''

Calder read one sentence, written at the top of the page. " 'Two hundred and fifty thousand years or so ago, New England was engulfed in the Siberian Winter.' Gran's got it on her mind because she keeps talking about it. She says she thinks the rock will be more impressive when it's out in the clear. Isn't that funny, Mr. Cooley? It's having it spring out at you, all of a sudden, that makes it tremendous.''

"I don't think your grandmother felt its presence.''

"But we three did. You and Walt and I!''

"Did it ever occur to you, Calder, that people are different?''

"Sure, but—''

"That's why you and Walt and I are in a league to protect the rock's hideout, and your grandmother is in a league to introduce tourists to the rock. By the way, have you seen Walt?''

She shook her head. "I've kept shop for Gran four afternoons this week. She's paying me for it. And it rained, and I finished *Wuthering Heights*. Do you think these fields are anything like the moors in *Wuthering Heights*, Mr. Cooley?''

110

"Not much."

"I hoped they were. In winter the wind must wuther, though."

"Oh, yes, I think you're safe there."

"You should have heard Walt tell about the winter. There were icicles as tall as he is hanging from their roof, and every morning almost he had to whack 'em down with a broomstick and jump out of the way because they could pierce right through you like daggers."

"You make me shudder. Did Walt describe them as daggers?"

"Why, yes—I don't know. They must have looked like daggers. Can't you see them!"

Mr. Cooley watched her face. "Yes, right there in your eyes. Do you think we ought to go up to the rock this afternoon and hold a meeting of the League? Say three o'clock. I have to get in my siesta."

"Shall we go the long way so the sign can point us to it?" Mr. Cooley asked, when they came up the road to the marker for the old town.

Calder hesitated. "I don't like it as well. I like the dogs barking and the mud sucking at your feet. It makes it sort of a 'passage perilous' to go through on our quest. But maybe we should see if Walt got all the rags down."

"The cemetery of the Balsam Saints," Mr. Cooley said, pointing Louie toward the gravestones.

"Oh, I do wish they could all rise up and come forth," Calder said. "A day like this. Wouldn't they love it! And they all must have known the rock, even the Revolutionary

soldiers, because it was here so long before they were."

"Ice ages before. The oldest rocks were millions of years old before the first living creatures appeared."

They came to a stop in front of the sign. "You know, it isn't bad looking, half hidden by the branch," Mr. Cooley said.

"And if it points without any path marked out, it won't take away from the quest so much."

"It most certainly won't," Mr. Cooley agreed. "You could still wander all over the hill and miss it."

"They're gone! Walt took the rags down!" Calder cried out joyously.

"The dogs may not hear us, and Walt won't know we're up here," Mr. Cooley suggested. But when they came to the wall, there was a bark, then another, then the usual storm of protest.

Mr. Cooley and Calder fell quiet, watching for the rock. There always seemed to be a waitingness about the woods, Calder thought. As though the woods were waiting to have them find it. When they came to the tree that was struck by lightning, Calder ran up the split branch. From there she could see the rock, not the wall between the trees, so much as the rounded top of it, but it was just as much of a surprise.

They climbed the rock. Mr. Cooley had more trouble than usual and was glad to take Calder's hand to pull himself up. "We might have a rustic ladder and hide it every time we leave," he said. "We'll have to take the matter up with the other member of the League. He and I could put one together."

They sat talking for half an hour, and still Walt didn't appear.

"I could go down far enough to start the dogs barking again," Calder offered.

"He may not be there. I suppose he does leave the farm sometimes."

"He's come every time before, even though he hid the first time I came."

Mr. Cooley looked surprised. "I thought the first time you came was the day we got Walt to bring us."

Calder blushed. "I didn't tell you, but I'd been here before. I didn't know anything about the rock. I just saw it suddenly through the trees. It scared me at first."

"How did you happen to come off up here alone?"

"I went for a hike in the first place, and then I crossed the field to get to these woods, and with the swamp and the dogs

113

barking, I didn't want to go back the same way. I thought maybe there'd be another road the other side of the hill.'' She looked at him anxiously. He must be thinking she was sneaky not to say she'd been here. But he was smiling.

"I thought I'd keep it secret—the rock, I mean. And then you came to dinner and showed the postcard with the rock on it. I didn't want to say anything then because Gran gets into such a fuss if I go off alone. I meant to tell you the next day, really I did. Then the next day I wanted to keep it secret, but I did feel underhanded.''

Mr. Cooley laughed. "There was nothing underhanded about it. I would say that you are one of those rare women who can keep their own counsel. You must have minded my making such an expedition of it, and no wonder you didn't like the idea of your grandmother's picnic!''

Calder pulled up her knees and hugged them in relief. "Oh, I'm so glad you know, Mr. Cooley. I felt terrible.''

"How did you know that Walt saw you?''

"When he stood up here on the rock and yelled that he was the King of the Mountain, remember? He'd seen me do that when I thought I was all alone. I was furious at him.''

Mr. Cooley laughed. "How much I missed! But you know, I remember thinking it was strangely out of character. He had struck me as such a quiet, almost surly boy. You are both more complicated than my colleagues on the faculty ever were. You fooled me completely.''

"Oh, don't say that, Mr. Cooley, please!'' Calder cried out. "Don't you see how it just happened? And you know everything now.'' She watched him anxiously until he said, "Calder, I quite understand your keeping the rock secret,

114

and I enjoy the thought of how completely you fooled me. Just so long as you don't put me out of the League!"

"We couldn't ever do that. You were the one who thought of having it."

"Walter!" Mr. Cooley exclaimed. "You came as quietly as an Indian."

Walter was standing below them. "Hi," he said, but there was something wrong Calder could see right away. He didn't make any move to climb up.

"We came the long way, and we were afraid the dogs didn't bark hard enough to let you know we were here. We saw you hadn't blazed the trail yet," Mr. Cooley said, expecting him to grin.

"Thanks for getting rid of all those red rags," Calder said.

"I knew you were up here," Walt said. He was the same silent boy he had been that first day, not really looking at them. He pulled off a pine needle and chewed it.

"Come on up, Walt. I have a project for the League," Mr. Cooley said. "I'm wondering if you and I couldn't make a ladder just for our own use and hide it when we leave each time."

Walt sat down on the ground against a pine tree. The lowest branch threw a shadow across his face. "I'm not coming up here any more. You can have the League by yourselves."

"What's the matter with you? Are you mad or something?" Calder sat cross-legged on top of the rock, looking down at him. The boy, with his head bent, went on digging at the ground with a stone he had brought out of his

115

pocket. He didn't answer or even look up.

"What's the matter, Walt?" Mr. Cooley asked gently.

"The rock isn't going to belong to us anymore. They're going to sell it," he blurted out, throwing the stone in his hand at the side of the rock.

"Who are going to sell it?" Mr. Cooley asked.

"Aunt Lil and my dad." For an instant, he glanced up, his face sullen in its hurt.

"Stop them! Tell them they mustn't," Calder said.

"Who are they going to sell it to, do you know?" Mr. Cooley asked.

Walt's head moved slowly. "Somebody from away. An' he's inter'sted in the wood lot, so he'll prob'ly cut all the trees down."

"That's awful! How can your father do that when he knows it has this rock on it? I thought he cared about the rock!"

Mr. Cooley touched Calder's arm and shook his head at her. He let himself down stiffly from the rock and sat on the ground beside Walter. "Your father and aunt must have their own reasons for selling, but Walt, their selling this wood lot won't ever take the rock away from you. You've made it yours. So has Calder. So have I, and we don't own it. You didn't mind sharing it with us, did you?"

"That's differ'nt. We still owned it. We could turn the dogs loose on anyone, if we wanted."

"But you didn't want to," Mr. Cooley said.

"She knew all the time. That's why she said she didn't care if they made a path in here," he burst out.

"Who? Oh, you mean your aunt. Walt, listen to me. One

116

of the troubles with the world is that people think they have to own things by deed instead of by their feeling about them and their knowledge and delight in them. I don't own a single bit of property any more, and I feel I own more than most people—all over the world. There's a place on the Chinese Wall in Montana that I feel I've made mine, and a jutting ledge on Mt. Hood that saved me once when I almost fell; that can't mean as much to anyone else as it does to me. There's even a place covered over now by the Nile that I think of as mine."

"But this is *mine,*" Walt burst in angrily, getting to his feet. "Mine and my folks. I got the right to say about it." He walked away from them without looking back. When he was a little distance, he began to run. They heard the dogs bark briefly and knew he was crossing the meadow. Calder stood up on the rock.

"I can't see him," she said. "Mr. Cooley, isn't that the meanest thing you ever heard of! How could his family do that?"

"They wouldn't do it hurriedly; perhaps they had to sell, but it is hard on Walt."

"Shall I go after him?"

"No. He wouldn't listen to you now."

"But I know how he feels. We sold our house; the place where I was born and lived all my life. It was the neatest place. We only did it because my mother and dad were divorced." Her eyes came back to Mr. Cooley. "I understand about that. They couldn't get along. Dad is erratic—like this boulder, and Mother is different. She has a regular job, and she likes to be with people and go places—but I hate not having our house and the pool and everything."

"I still miss the house I was born in," Mr. Cooley said, "although I'm so old you'll find that's hard to believe. But you know it's true that we don't really lose places we've made ours."

Calder shook her head. "That isn't any good, Mr. Cooley. It's a nice idea, but it isn't the real nitty-gritty truth." She slid down from the rock, and they started back the way they had come.

"If I owned this rock, nothing in the world would make me sell it," Calder burst out. "Nothing!"

Mr. Cooley was silent.

When they came to the sign, Calder said, "Going to the rock will never be the same."

"But the rock will be," Mr. Cooley said. "For the next few centuries, anyway. It was wrenched out of its home, too, you remember, and knocked about, and scraped over ledges, and dragged into a completely strange terrain before it finally found its angle of repose on this Vermont hillside—" He broke off because Calder didn't seem to be listening.

11

Calder hadn't been listening to Mr. Cooley. She was deciding that she would go to see Walt. She couldn't let him just go off like that; he felt terrible. Besides, there must be something he could do to stop their selling the land with the rock on it. She thought about it all through dinner.

"I can't eat my pie, Mardie. Can I save it?"

"Of course, dear, but for a girl who has been on a long hike, I don't think you have a very good appetite."

Calder let the remark go. "As soon as I dry the dishes, I'm going out on my bike. Barb and all of them will be out," she said vaguely, but it was perfectly true; they were out on their bikes nearly every evening.

"Then go right along without drying the dishes, but be

back by nine. I like to have you feel free as the air, Calder. For, after all, that's what it means to live in a small Vermont village."

Calder murmured her thanks and ran out of the house. She knew people now in Weldon. Everyone thought of her as the Calder girl. "Hi," she said to Mr. Kerr, sitting on his porch. "Good evening," she called to Mrs. Stebbins, turning carefully off the walk for her. But she kept a lookout for Barbie and the crowd. It wouldn't be easy to explain why she was shooting off alone up the Old Town Road. Barbie would know that she was going to see Walt, and kid her. When she did see Barbie, she made a big swoop on the main street and threw her bicycle against the big urn of geraniums on the front lawn of the library.

"Going to the libe?" Barb called out.

"What does it look like?" Calder called back, already half way up the steps. She'd have to get a book now to make it honest. But once in the library, she was drawn to the books in spite of herself. *Vanity Fair* was next on her school reading list, but it looked awfully fat and old-fashioned. Then she saw *Love Story* in a brand new cover on the front table. That was in the movies—but you never got to the movies up here. She took it to the librarian's desk. The librarian looked surprised. "Is this for your grandmother, Calder? I don't believe she's next on the waiting list. No, Mrs. Baxter is next." She seemed relieved. "Would you like to pick out a book for yourself? We have some fine new books over there on the adolescent shelf. You can take a book out on your grandmother's card."

"No, thank you," Calder said. She didn't really want to

carry a book up there anyway, but she would come back and get that *Love Story* book another time. It looked little enough to read, standing right there, if she couldn't take it out.

The road was clear when she came out, and she could whirl up the middle of the street to the hill road, unnoticed. She could go farther now without stopping, but she had to stand on her pedals and pump for all she was worth. It was slick riding at the top of the hill where the road leveled off and the sky was all pink over the the tops of the trees.

As she came in sight of the Bolles' farm, the dogs began. Their barking coming out of the dark, closed barn seemed loud enough to hear all the way in town. Nobody was on the porch of Walt's aunt's house, but there was a light in the kitchen. His aunt would wonder why she had come up here at night if she just rode into the yard, so she went past the house, far enough so that the barking stopped. Then she dropped her bike on the ground and perched on the stone wall. It would be more fun to go up to the rock because she had never been there at night, but Walt might not come. It hurt him too much. She knew how he felt. She wasn't going back to their house when she got back, either. Or, if she did, she wouldn't really look at her special places. Maybe Walt wouldn't even come out. He might have thought it was just someone going by. But he must have looked out. Maybe he wouldn't want to see her. She sat still, waiting. The small peeping sounds of birds and the chill of the growing dusk gave the evening a lonesome feeling.

There he was, coming down the road, droop-shouldered, hands in his jeans, his face white in the dusk. He was walking slow, as though he didn't want to come.

"Whaddya want?" He didn't act surprised that she had come, but not mad either.

"Walt, I felt so terrible about your family selling the place. I know what it's like—"

He shrugged. "It's O.K. I don't really care. I'm going to school in town."

That stopped her for a minute. Then she knew it wasn't true, any more than what Mr. Cooley said about not really ever losing a place was true.

"Can't you do something about it?"

Walt sat down on the wall, but his face was turned away from her so that he looked up toward the woods and the rock. "I'd just like to talk to my dad, but he's in the hospital."

"Why don't you go to see him? You ought to talk to him!"

"I'm going to see him when Aunt Lil takes the papers to sign."

"But it will be too late then! Maybe he doesn't know how important the rock is or that you don't want him to sell it." Her voice came out of the slow twilight with sharp intensity. "Why don't you go to see him right away?"

"He's way over in Truxton."

"How far is that?"

"Forty or fifty miles, maybe more."

"Why, that's nothing! You could go easy, tomorrow."

He gave a scornful laugh. "Are you crazy? You mean ride my bike all that way?"

"No, that would take too long. You can hitchhike." She

thought about asking Mardie to drive him, but gave the idea up at once as impractical. "You're sure to get rides the whole way." She was a little surprised at herself. She had never hitchhiked. Mother would have been furious if she ever did, and Dad would tell her he'd skin her alive; but, of course, it was different here in the country. Mardie was always telling her how much safer Vermont was than California.

Walt was silent, but the idea seemed to be taking root. "I'd sure like to talk to my dad," he said.

"Then go!" Calder urged. "They're more apt to pick you up if you're" —she had been going to say just a kid, but she changed it to— "not grown up, and specially, if you don't look like a hippy. What could you tell your aunt?"

Walt considered. "Maybe I could say the ball team was going some place for the day. She's good about letting me do things, only there isn't much to do here."

Calder thought it over. "It would be a lie, and she might find out, but I guess it's the best thing you can think of. After all, it *is* a crisis. You ought to get started by eight."

"I could get done with chores by then, easy."

"And ride down on your bike and leave it at our house. You need to look slicked up and kind of beaming to get picked up." She hated to say it, but Walt could look so droopy and cross sometimes. "I wish Mr. Cooley had a car," she added.

"What if I don't get picked up?"

"Well, you will, of course. Have you ever been there before?"

He nodded. "It's a great big place. You can go in only at

123

the right times.''

''You're sure to be there for them, if you leave here at eight.''

''Aunt Lil will wonder why I just remembered about the ball game.''

''Goodness! You've had enough to think about to put that out of your mind until just now. She'll know that. Maybe she'll be glad to get your mind off the sale.''

He looked uncertain.

''And tell your dad about the rock and how valuable it is—that people think it's a natural wonder and want to make a path to it.''

''He knows all about the rock.''

''My dad does, too. He wrote me a card from England about it. I guess nobody who's seen it ever forgets the rock.''

They heard his aunt calling, making two syllables of his name. ''Wa-alt!''

''I gotta go. I'll think about it. I'm not sure.''

''You're crazy if you don't. It's easy as anything. You go on; I'll wait a minute.''

Calder waited until she heard the screen door bang before she got on her bike. She rode past the barking dogs, past the turn-off to the cemetery of Saints, through the place where the trees made a dark tunnel. The light on her bicycle picked out sudden spots: a fern turned yellow in the brightness, a gray patch on a dark tree trunk, and birch trees, whiter than in daylight. The ruts in the road were like chocolate ridges on a frosting bowl. When she came out of the tunnel, the fields between their stone walls still held some light. A bat

124

flew past her and came back again before it dived off into the dark. It was lovely riding along on top of the hill, past the house with its one tiny light; lovelier still when the road swooped downhill, and she could coast all the way into town.

"Did you have a good time, dear? I was just beginning to worry," Gran called.

"Hmm. I mean yes, Mardie. I'm hungry though. I guess I'll eat my pie."

12

Calder woke early the next morning with the feeling of something momentous about to happen—not necessarily super, like going to a play or to the beach for the whole day; quite the opposite, something ominous, like going to the dentist or taking an examination. Her eyes moved up the green-sprigged wallpaper of her room to the wavy plaster of the ceiling that ran out over the small-paned windows in the two gables. A trip, that was it, but Walt's not hers. Would he really go or would he chicken out?

She threw back the covers and dressed quickly, putting on her tie-dyed jeans that had the wonderful streaks of red and white all over them; they made her feel equal to anything. If Walt didn't come by, she would go up there and talk to him some more. Her orange turtle-neck made her feel brave, too. Gran called the combination her California outfit and said it set her teeth on edge. Calder braided her hair and fastened the ends with her strongest elastic bands.

She was glad they ate breakfast so early, so she was free to keep watch for Walt. "Would you like me to take Viva out for her walk, Mardie?" Calder asked as soon as she was through putting the breakfast dishes away.

"Oh, yes, dear, that's very nice of you. Take her all around the common. Take her leash!" Calder was always letting her run without it.

Just as she came out the front gate, she saw Walt riding slowly along the other side of the common and knew he must have gone by their house once already. She waved and he came around. Viva barked at him in her high, thin bark that made Walt laugh. He was going, she could see. He was all slicked up; people would be sure to give him a lift.

He sat on his bike, but he reached down to pat Viva. "Hi," he said.

"Hi. Come on, I'll show you where to put your bike, back of the lilac bush so nobody'll see it." She went ahead, he followed. "Did you have trouble telling your aunt?"

"I told her a plain lie," he said soberly.

"Well, you had to because it's a crisis."

"I told her the team was going to play in Brattleboro, an' they needed everyone, an' that there was going to be someone to drive us there." He looked miserable over what he had done. "Aunt Lil wouldn't ever think I'd lie."

"When you're back home, you can tell her and she'll

forgive you," Calder said briskly. "You ought to get going now. The sooner you're on the road, the better. I stopped last night at the gas station on my way back, and asked Mr. Hollis how far it is to Truxton. He said it was about forty miles."

"Of course, you know that's eighty miles both ways! I was thinking that it isn't going to do any good anyhow because my dad's already told Aunt Lil he'll sell."

Calder was impatient at his having qualms now. She stood behind the lilac bush, breaking off the green, heart-shaped leaves. "Don't you want to make a *try* anyhow to hold on to the rock? How many kids own a rock like that? And if my dad was sick, I'd *walk* miles and miles just to go and talk to him."

"If nobody picks me up, I'll just have to come back, I suppose."

He looked so discouraged already, before he had even started out, that she made up her mind. "Walt, I'm going with you. You wait here behind the lilac bush till I go in and leave a note. I don't want to have to talk to Mardie now." Without waiting for an answer she was racing across the lawn, Viva barking as she ran. With relief, she noticed that Mardie was in the shop. On the pad Mardie kept in the kitchen, she wrote:

"Dearest Mardie:" She wet the point of her pencil trying to think what was best to say. "Going on a lovely expedition with the kids. Someone's taking us in a car. I won't be back till dark, prob'ly. Don't wait dinner and don't worry. Tell you all when I return. Bushels of love, Calder."

That would have to do. It was nearly true; she was going with *one* kid, and *someone* would be taking them in a car. She raced up to her room and took the three dollars left of her earnings this month, folded them into a small enough square to push into the tight little pocket under her belt, then hurried back to the lilac bush.

"It's sure funny just walking out of town like this. How soon are you going to try for a lift?" Walt asked.

"Any minute now. All right, there's a car. Hold up your thumb and smile. You have to look as though you'd be fun to have along."

The car went by without slackening speed.

"Lots of them will go by, but there's no end of cars," Calder said cheerfully.

A truck drew to a stop beside them. "Hop in. How far you going?" the driver asked. Calder considered quickly and decided that their actual destination was too far to say. She wished she had looked at the map so she knew the names of all the towns along the way, but Walt spoke up. "Spencer."

"Well now, it just happens I'm going through Spencer, so I can drop you right there. That's quite a distance for you two kids to start out and walk to." He was a friendly looking man. Calder felt triumphant. They settled down on the high slippery seat.

"This is swell," Walt said.

"We surely appreciate your stopping," Calder added.

"You have friends in Spencer or just going for the sights?"

The question took them unprepared. Neither of them

wanted to tell a lie unnecessarily. Calder decided to take a chance, the driver was so nice.

"We want to go farther than that really, to the Veterans Hospital at Truxton."

"Well, sir, you're in luck because I'm going close to there on the Thruway. You can see the hospital from where I let you out. You got someone sick there?"

"My Dad." Walt felt better since everything was working out so well. "Gee, that's great." And then Walt asked a question that he'd been wanting to ask. "How many horse-power has this engine got?" They were great friends by the time the driver let them off.

"Imagine having as good as a taxi ride right to it! See, it's easy as falling off a log," Calder exulted. But as they went up the long flight of steps to the imposing entrance, she was more meek. "It's good you've been here before." The clock back of the long desk said ten-fifteen.

"You want to see Mr. Bolles?" The woman at the desk asked. "Is he your father?"

"Yes, sir; I mean ma'am."

"We don't usually let children visit the wards by themselves." She pointed to a sign on the desk. "And visiting hours are not until one o'clock."

Walt's eyes were fixed on hers. "I hitchhiked forty miles over here. I need to ask my father something—something important. It won't take long."

The woman consulted a file. Then she talked over the phone, speaking very low, but Walt heard her say "depressed—well, maybe it would cheer him up." When she hung up, she said to Walt with a smile, "You look about sixteen. You wait till eleven o'clock. Then you go up to the fourth floor, down at the end of the hall, and give the nurse at the desk this card. And don't stay more than ten minutes!''

"Thank you," Walt said.

Calder was waiting on a bench in the lobby. When Walt turned away from the desk, she came toward him.

"We gotta wait till eleven, so we might as well go back and sit down. They don't let children go in alone," Walt told her. "But she said I looked about sixteen." He grinned, watching the effect on Calder.

She wished she had worn something more grownup.

"That's what she said." Walt sat up straighter.

After that, there didn't seem to be much to talk about, so they sat silent, watching the people and the clock.

On the stroke of eleven, Walt led the way to the elevator and grandly pushed the button. When they got out at the fourth floor, he showed his card. Calder was proud of him. She guessed he could have managed all right by himself. Men were walking down the hall in bathrobes; a man went by in a wheel chair; another man was being wheeled by on a kind of table. When they came to a big room full of men in beds, Calder hung back.

"I'll wait out here." She stood in the doorway long enough to watch Walt go over to the bed in the corner. The man sitting up against the pillows was surprised, then he smiled. He looked a little like Walt. She stepped back into the hall and sat down on the bench near the desk. Even in that glance she had seen two things: that the man was glad to see Walt and that he looked sicker than anybody she had ever seen before.

There were so many sick men going by it was a relief to see the doctors in white coats with stethoscopes around their necks or sticking out of their pockets. They looked like the doctors in "The Interns" she watched on TV—if Dad wasn't around. They walked briskly and sometimes laughed. The nurses looked healthy, too, and moved fast. One of them smiled at her as she passed.

Calder watched the elevator open and people get out and in and the lights coming on over closed doors down the hall. It got to be quarter of twelve before Walt came back. He looked awfully serious.

"We might as well go," he said.

Calder rose obediently. When they were in the elevator, Walt said, "There's a cafeteria in the basement where we can get something to eat before we go back."

"I have my own money," Calder said.

"I have, too." Walt blushed.

But if this wasn't a date, Calder thought, as she followed Walt into the cafeteria, she didn't know what was: having lunch alone with a boy in a public restaurant. She selected orange juice, a sticky bun, and cocoa. Walt took pancakes, sausage, and milk. Calder decided she needed something more and went back through the long line to get an order of sausage by itself. Gran didn't ever have it. Calder and Walt paid for their own orders.

Walt had eaten most of his pancakes before he said, "Dad was sure glad to see me."

"Natch," Calder said, a little self-righteously for having thought up the trip.

133

"But he says he'll be there—in dry-dock, he calls it—for a while yet. He thinks we oughta sell the farm." Walt pushed a forkful of pancake around in the syrup on his plate without looking up. "His part of the money is going into the bank for me for college. He says that's the important thing."

Calder stopped eating. "What about the rock? Did you tell him how you felt about it?"

Walt nodded. "I didn't have to tell him anything. He used to go there all the time when he was a kid. I told him about Mr. Cooley and you and the League. It made him laugh till he coughed."

"Didn't that make him want to keep it?"

Walt was slow in answering. "He said the rock would still be there when I got through college. Maybe I could buy the place back some day."

Calder was silent. She had been so sure that Walt's father would tell him to tell his aunt not to sell.

"He says it isn't fair to Aunt Lil not to sell."

Grownups always had reasons. They didn't really listen to yours. Walt's coming hadn't done any good then, except for seeing his dad. And Gran was going to raise a big stink about her going off. She lifted the scum off the cocoa with her spoon. She had put in too much sugar, and it was too sweet. She wondered how she'd tell Walt she had to go to the ladies' room before they started back. She could see where it was. Mardie always called it the "little girls' room," which sounded pretty silly. "I'll be back," she said, and left quickly.

Walt was waiting in the doorway to the cafeteria. "I

guess I'll just go and see if I can tell Dad good-by,'' he said. ''You can wait out front on the steps, if you want.''

People didn't stop for them on the Thruway. They were driving too fast to see them. Even the trucks went by. It was scary walking on the edge with cars coming so close to them. They couldn't talk because Walt stalked ahead and she was behind him.

''Try the next three,'' Calder shouted at his back.

They stood still and held out their arms with their thumbs pointed up and smiled. After the third car had passed them by, Walt started to walk again. Calder followed. She felt as though they had walked two miles. When they came to the Rest Area, she suggested stopping. ''Somebody'll pick us up here easier, because they aren't really supposed to stop on the Thruway. Look!'' Calder pointed to the green trash can with ''Keep Vermont Beautiful'' painted on it.

''Yeah. It'd look great, wouldn't it! And a space around the rock all marked off with logs like this.''

There was only one car parked there. The man who sat in it opened his door and smiled at them. ''You kids want a ride?'' he asked.

''No, thank you,'' Calder answered quickly. ''Come on, Walt. We have to hurry if we're going to meet our folks.''

''I'll drive you as far as you're going,'' the man said. ''Get in.''

Calder began to run. She didn't know why. Something about the man's toothy smile frightened her. He didn't have a real beard like Dad's, but a black unshaven fringe on his chin. His mouth or his eyes—something about his face—was horrid.

"Say, what's the matter with you?" Walt caught up with her. "Did you hear him say he'd take us all the way to where we're going?"

"I didn't like his looks. I wouldn't get in his old car for anything."

"He'll be coming along and see we aren't meeting anyone."

"We can turn off the first exit and go into a town. It ought to be easier off the Thruway."

"You're nuts," Walt said. "Now we may have to walk miles. And it's getting hot."

They tramped along in silence except for the whizzing of the cars. Calder was in the lead.

"Here's one that's going kinda slow," Walt said. They stopped, held out their arms with thumbs pointed. Calder smiled. A woman driving the car waved at them and went on by. Neither of them made any comment. Calder started on.

"You know what?" Walt said, "Dad wants me to chip a piece off the rock and bring it to him. I'm going to get a good-sized one. He says he'll keep it on the window right by his bed."

"I might send a piece to my dad," Calder said. Then she remembered that he was in England, but she could save it for him till he got back.

As they came to the exit sign, the man from the Rest Area drove by and slowed down, honking at them.

"Keep going and pretend not to hear him," Calder muttered. They turned off the exit road at a rapid walk. "I hate Thruways,'' Calder said. "But this is only a little two-horse one. You should see the ones in California. They're a hundred thousand times scarier. I wouldn't dare walk on one of them.'' Walt didn't answer. "It's only a quarter after two,'' Calder said. "We've got lots of time.'' She felt he needed cheering.

"Not if we have to walk the whole way, we haven't. Let's try in front of this gasoline station.''

A pick-up truck coming out of the station stopped. "I'm going to Spencer. You want to go there?'' The driver was a young man with a load of plywood. "You know they patrol this road. If a cop sees you hitchhiking, he's liable to really pick you up.'' But he said it with a grin.

"Oh, thank you for saving us,'' Calder said.

Walt scowled at her actressy tone of voice. "Thanks,'' he said gruffly.

"Where you headed for? You haven't said yet.''

"Home,'' Calder said.

"To Weldon,'' Walt added.

"Oh, well, you ought to get a lift over from Spencer. Where you been to?''

"To the hospital to make a sick call,'' Calder told him.

Walt didn't like the way she was always getting her two cents worth in before he got a chance. He wished he'd come alone instead of having a girl tagging along. He didn't like her saying they'd gone on a sick call, either.

"D'you hitchhike all the way over this morning?''

Walt hurried to answer before she could. "Yeah, but a big truck picked us up and took us all the way there.''

"Say now, that was a break! Sorry I can't take you all the

way home." As they came into Spencer, the driver said, "Look's like your sister's all in."

Calder had fallen asleep, her head against the driver's arm. Walt poked her. He let the sister stand; it wasn't as bad as girl-friend would be.

"Leave her be," the driver said.

"Oh, I guess I fell asleep. Walking in the sun always makes me sleepy," Calder said, sitting up straight, blinking her eyes to get awake.

"I'll leave you here at the shopping plaza; that ought to be a good place to catch a lift the rest of the way," the driver said.

"Thanks," they chorused, as he drove off.

"I'll get home in plenty of time to do chores," Walt said. "I'll have to tell Aunt Lil the truth. Dad said I should."

"I'm not going to tell Gran. She'd be horrified. I may tell Mr. Cooley and ask him if I can say I decided I didn't want to go with the kids and went on a rock-hunting expedition with him." The brilliant thought had just occurred to her.

Walt looked at her. "Say, you're the biggest liar I ever knew. You just make up one after another. I never would have thought of doing this in the first place if you hadn't had the idea."

"What do you think I had the idea for?"

"I didn't ask you to. You came up last night of your own free will."

They were so busy arguing that they didn't see the car stop by them, as they stood holding their thumbs out at the entrance to the parking space.

"Why, Calder Bailey, whatever are you doing? Do you

138

mean to say you're hitchhiking?''

To Calder's horror, the woman was one of the friends Mardie was always going antiquing with. "Oh, hello, Mrs. Canby. Well, yes, we do need a ride back to Weldon."

"Get right in. And you're the Bolles boy, aren't you? What on earth are you children doing?''

Walt let himself into the back seat and was silent. Calder sat in front. She pulled at her pigtail for inspiration. "We—we were bicycling and my bicycle broke down, so we thought we'd hitchhike back." She could feel Walt's eyes on the back of her head. He'd call her a worse liar.

"I see. Where are your bicycles? Maybe we could put them in the trunk."

"Oh, they're—we left them at the—at a service station to be fixed."

"You mean you rode on your bicycles all the way over here!''

"Well, no, not exactly. We were on the road, and a truck with a very nice driver picked us up and brought us here." It was a relief to have part of her story true.

"But you must have gone as far as the road to Spencer then. That's quite far from home!''

"I'm used to bicycling for miles in California," Calder said.

"Well, you poor dear, I'm certainly glad I came along," Mrs. Canby said. "Your grandmother would have been beside herself with worry, if she'd known about it."

Calder's spirits, which had begun to revive with the movement of the car toward home, fell to the bottom of her feet. Mrs. Canby would tell Gran all she'd told her.

139

"Mardie tells me you're having a wonderful summer, climbing the hills and visiting Serpentine Rock, and doing the things you can only do in Vermont!"

"Yes, I'm having a fine time," Calder said.

"And I hear that you're making us a trail up to Serpentine." Mrs. Canby looked in the mirror to see Walt. He was gazing out the side of the car and didn't seem to hear.

"Mrs. Canby's talking to you, Walt!" Calder said.

"Uh, yes, ma'am. I'm going to. I haven't got it done yet."

So! Walt was a liar too, because he didn't mean to at all. Calder turned around to smile at him, but he looked away.

Calder wondered if it would be best to throw herself on Mrs. Canby's mercy and ask her not to tell Gran she had been hitchhiking or even that she had ever picked them up. She studied her profile, trying to decide whether Mrs. Canby was the kind of grownup who could be trusted. They were almost home.

Mrs. Canby slowed suddenly. "Look at that lovely Deacon's bench on that porch! I've been by here hundreds of times, and I've never noticed it before. I wonder if they'd sell it. Anyway, I must tell Mardie about it."

Calder hated the thought of Walt's hearing her beg Mrs. Canby not to tell. Her hands felt cold, and she put them under her. Mrs. Canby saw the movement and looked down.

"Those are the most spectacular pants I think I've ever seen, Calder! Did you tie-dye them yourself?"

"Yes," Calder said. "Everyone wears them at home. I

140

mean, everyone my age.'' It seemed a long time since morning when she had put them on to give her courage for the day.

"I thought they looked like California!'' Mrs. Canby said in that superior tone of voice Gran used when she talked about California. They were driving into Weldon. It was too late to tell Mrs. Canby anything. Calder pulled her hands out from under her, but they were no warmer.

Mrs. Canby drove around the common and stopped in Gran's driveway. Of course, Gran would be right there, airing Viva!

"Where do you suppose I picked up these two waifs, Mardie?'' Mrs. Canby called out.

"Thanks,'' Walt muttered, and went streaking across the lawn to the lilac bush. Calder watched him ride past, not caring that Mrs. Canby would see his bike. He didn't even look as he went by.

"Calder, *where* have you been?'' Mardie asked. "I've puzzled all day over your note. And why would you go anywhere in a costume like that!''

"Oh, Gran, it'll take too long to explain now. I'll run up and take a bath. Thank you ever so much, Mrs. Canby.'' She disappeared gratefully into the cool house. From her window, she heard Mrs. Canby driving away, and Mardie calling out, "Well, I do thank you. I'm going to have quite a talk with Calder.''

Calder took a long time in the bath tub. In the hot soapy water, she stopped feeling scared. She would simply go down and tell Mardie the truth. She couldn't possibly make up another lie. After she got out of the tub, she brushed her

141

teeth hard, as though to cleanse her mouth of every big and little lie. They were all for Walt, and then he had turned around and called her a liar. She put on her blue pique dress Mardie had sent her last Christmas and Mother had said to be sure to wear often and brushed her hair until most of the kinks from braiding it were smoothed out, and tied a pale blue ribbon around her head. Then she slowly descended the stairs.

Mardie was in the kitchen. "How nice you look, dear." Mardie's voice was dangerously sweet.

"Can I help—I mean, may I?" Calder asked.

"No, thank you. I thought you must be hungry after your 'lovely expedition' so we would have an early dinner."

Mardie was using the words from her note. "I am," Calder said.

"Why don't you go out and rest on the porch swing until dinner's ready, Calder." Mardie began to hum in a way that dismissed her. It would have been better if she'd been cross and begun to scold her right away. Calder lay on the swing, but she didn't bother to set it in motion. It seemed to be taking Mardie a long time to get dinner. She got up and went back to the kitchen.

"Could I pour your sherry for you, Mardie, and get a glass of ginger ale for me?"

There was a little pause, as though Gran was considering, then she said, "Why, yes, Calder, if you will please." But Gran's tone was still chilly sweet. It changed when they were both sitting on the porch, each with her glass.

"Well, Calder, suppose you tell me what you were up to. You know, I've treated you like an adult whom I could trust. I wrote your mother that she should be proud of you, but I find I was wrong. How, pray, did you happen to go off with that Bolles boy?''

If it were only Dad instead of Gran, he would say, ''Calder Chimpanzee Bailey'' —which was one of his lowest epithets— ''what fine piece of villainy were you up to?'' Or Mother would say, ''Lambie child, what got into you?'' And she could tell them anything, and maybe cry, and be forgiven and comforted, and it would all be over. But Gran was different. She hated Gran's voice.

''Well, I—'' She swallowed. Gran had put down her sherry glass and was looking right at her. ''It all began because Walt heard that his aunt and his father are selling the farm.''

''You seem to be pretty closely involved with the Bolles' affairs.''

Calder ignored Gran's remark. ''And that means they'll sell the wood lot with the rock in it, Serpentine Rock, Gran.'' Gran's face showed no interest in the rock, after all the fuss she had made about it. Calder plunged on. ''He felt terrible when he told Mr. Cooley and me about it; he was nearly crying. I didn't see him, but I could tell,'' she put in, so that she would not deviate in the slightest degree from the truth. ''So—I asked him if he couldn't go to see his father and tell him how he wanted to keep the rock in the family.'' It wasn't quite honest to let Gran think she had asked him right then, but there was no use telling her she had ridden up there last night when Gran thought she had been with Barbie. It seemed hopeless to get *every* lie straightened out.

''I would hardly think, Calder, that you had any right to

143

mix up with a family matter."

"It was only that I felt so bad for him. And about the rock, too."

"I see."

"And Walt said his father was in the Veterans' Hospital and he didn't know how he could get there"—she took a breath—"so I said he could hitchhike there."

"Calder Bailey, that's a most dangerous thing to do! Furthermore, it's illegal to pick up hitchhikers. I would never, never stop for anyone."

Calder waited. "But this morning when Walt came down here to leave his bike—"

"I didn't see any bike. Where did he leave it?"

"Behind the lilac bush so it wouldn't be in the way."

"Please attempt to tell the truth, Calder. You mean, so that I wouldn't see it."

"He seemed so hopeless about everything that I"—Calder braced herself inwardly—"I said I'd go with him."

"Calder Vanderbush Bailey!" Gran's face was red.

Calder waited, but Gran didn't say anything more. "A very courteous truck driver picked us up and drove us all the way to the Veterans' Hospital."

"And I suppose that you went in to see Mr. Bolles, too!"

Gran's voice was hateful. "No, I waited outside the room. He's very sick, I think, Gran. And Walt—Walter was glad he'd gone to see him. But Mr. Bolles said they have to sell the farm. So then we came home. A young man in a pick-up took us to that big shopping place, and Mrs. Canby brought us from there. That's all there is to it. I'm sorry, Gran; I won't ever hitchhike again."

Gran sat still, as though she were going over everything in her mind. "What distresses me very much, Calder, was your leaving a note that was intended to deceive me."

"No, Gran, that isn't *quite* so. Of course, I knew you wouldn't let me go if I asked you, and I wanted to help Walt, but I only said that about going on a lovely expedition so you wouldn't worry. It was really for your sake." It was such a relief to get it all out, she didn't care what Gran said or how she punished her. She hoped Gran wouldn't make her go to bed without dinner, just when it was all ready and smelling so good.

Gran was silent so long, Calder looked over at her. Something terrible had happened to Gran's face. Her mouth was trembling. Why she was crying!

"Gran!" Calder said in amazement.

"Calder, Calder, don't you see. I was so sure I could trust you completely, and then you lied to me and went off like one of those dreadful common adolescents that you read about. You even looked like one of them—with a boy you hardly knew. And did a dangerous thing like that!"

"Oh, Gran, don't cry. I'm not a dreadful adolescent who takes grass and stuff, even if I did look like one. And you can trust me." It was terrible. She would rather have Gran the cold, hateful way she was at first.

"Calder!" Gran cried out as though she was in pain or something. "Why would you say a word like that? Where did you ever hear of—of 'grass'?"

"Why, I guess I read about it in the paper, and it's on TV; everybody at school talks about it. I asked Dad, and he told me it was what sad people took who had nothing in

145

their heads, like imagination or eyes to see with, or anything.''

Mrs. Calder dropped the subject. "When I think, Calder, how I told your mother you would be so safe here—and you might have—" Gran's words were choked in her crying, real sobs. Calder didn't know what to do.

"Gran, you can punish me as hard as you want, but please, please don't cry. I can't stand it.''

"Calder, I want the truth: it was just as you said; nothing else happened?''

"Yes, Gran, truly. Cross my heart and hope to die! We were lucky to get those long rides.''

Gran wiped her eyes. "You were very lucky. And you won't ever do such a terrible thing again? You won't go anywhere for the rest of the summer without asking me?''

Calder hesitated. "Gran, you said you wanted me to feel free up here. I promise I won't do anything stupid like that again, but please don't make me come and ask you about everything I do.''

Gran looked at her a long time. It was hard to look back at Gran, because her face was so crumpled, sort of. "All right, Calder. I'll trust you once more.''

And then it was easy. Calder rushed over and hugged her. "Oh, Gran, you don't know how good it is to be in the clear again and feel honest. And could we eat now?''

"My darling child, of course! You must be starved. Where did you eat?''

Halfway through the meal, Calder laid her fork down on her plate. "For punishment, Gran, I won't go beyond the fence for three whole days. Dad and Mother often let me think up my own punishments. I've had lots of practice and I'm pretty good at it. Dad always says, 'Let the punishment fit the crime.' Do you think that would? Because I really abused my freedom, and I did lie, and yet what Dad calls my motivation wasn't bad, was it? I mean, it was all to help someone in sore trouble.''

"I guess that might do," Mardie said weakly. She felt suddenly too old to bring up a child Calder's age.

13

Calder had stayed for three days within the garden, bounded like a prison by the bars of the picket fence. Time dragged. Mardie had gone to the Inn for dinner with friends both nights, and Calder had eaten alone.

"They wanted to include you, Calder, but I told them you had chosen to stay home," Gran had explained.

"Did you tell them why?" Calder minded having strangers know about her sins.

"I told them you were exhausted by a rather strenuous expedition you went on."

The house had seemed very empty in the evening, even though Gran hadn't stayed late; Viva was so nervous that she barked at the least little noise.

The second evening, Gran had come home all excited about someone she had met, "who was greatly interested, of all things, Calder, in the rock. He has an astounding idea, but I won't say anything about it yet." Calder didn't ask. If Gran wanted to be so mysterious, let her.

Keeping shop had helped to pass some of the time, but this afternoon Mardie wanted to be there herself, because she thought she had a customer for the cherry chest that was one of her best and most expensive pieces of furniture.

Calder lay in the hammock. Gran did have one of Dad's novels—just the first one—but she said it was too old for her. Dad said nothing was too old for her to try; in books, he meant. So she had brought it down to the garden to begin next. It was called *A Pigmy's Straw* and Dad's name was there on the outside in gold and inside on the center of the page. Suddenly, she was afraid the novel would be sad. She couldn't stand that just now. She let the book lie on her stomach and lay staring up through the maple trees.

She thought about her lying; she could never explain to anybody that she didn't set out to lie; it was just that answers occurred to her sometimes that seemed to make things better all round. But then they didn't.

When she heard the latch on the gate click, she hung out of the hammock to see if it was only another visitor to the shop. To her great relief, there was Mr. Cooley coming right past the shop down to the garden.

"Hello!" Mr. Cooley waved Louie at her and came on across the lawn. " 'This lime-tree bower thy prison is'."

"There are only maples and one elm and two apple trees," Calder told him. "You're thinking of California."

149

"Lime tree is just a manner of speaking. It comes from a poem by a man who wanted to go on a long walk with some friends, but he had to stay home because of a sore foot, so the shady bower under the lime tree became a prison even though it was beautiful. The man's name was Samuel Coleridge. Are visitors allowed in your prison bower?"

"We didn't say anything about visitors, and I'm so thankful you came. I feel as though I'd been in prison for weeks!"

Mr. Cooley laid Louie on the ground and sat down in the awning chair by the hammock. "You look like a very cheerful prisoner."

"Oh, once you've decided to wear the hair-shirt of penance, you must wear it cheerfully, Dad says."

"But that doesn't keep the hair-shirt from being prickly on a warm day like this."

"No, and I'm sick of it. But I can get rid of it tomorrow. Mr. Cooley, do you always know when you're lying? I mean, right at the moment you're saying something that isn't quite true."

"Well, yes. I think I do know." Mr. Cooley looked grave. When he looked grave, he looked old. She had never noticed before how his face was criss-crossed with fine wrinkles like the thin lines on the rock. Her eyes studied his face so they could escape from the steady look of his eyes.

"Have you been to the rock?" she asked quickly.

"I wouldn't think of going to the rock without you. You're the one who goes without me! I went up that hill over there to the old quarry hole." Mr. Cooley fished in his pocket. "Here, I brought you a piece of soapstone that's related to serpentine."

Calder fingered the smooth surface with one finger. "It doesn't look like it, really."

"Do you and all your cousins look exactly alike?"

"Well, no."

"I wondered if you would like to celebrate your freedom tomorrow by going to the quarry?"

"I think I'd rather go to the rock and see where Walt chipped off a piece for his father. Besides, I want to know whether his aunt was awfully mad at him."

So the next afternoon Mr. Cooley and Louie and Calder set off up the hill.

"It does smooth out your mind to come up this hill out of town, doesn't it?" Calder said as they stopped for Mr. Cooley to get his breath.

"Yes, it does, Calder. I know exactly what you mean. Looking at rocks does, too."

At the crossroads, they took the old cemetery road down to the sign-board and climbed over the wall without any comment, then turned up the sloping field toward the wood lot beyond the next wall.

"I find it a relief not to have those hounds barking," Mr. Cooley said.

"Yes, except that the barking does make you feel excited. And the other way is so much shorter."

151

Mr. Cooley gave a low whistle. "Do you see what I see, Calder?"

Calder's eyes moved quickly ahead through the fringe of woods. Then she saw. On a tree near the wall, a clean white arrow had been cut deep into the bark. Drops of sap beaded the cuts. Calder ran ahead and found a similar arrow cut this time into a white birch tree. She waited for Mr. Cooley to catch up with her. Not quite speaking aloud, she said, "Why would he do that? If he was really forced to it, he said he was going to make the blazes so light that they'd grow over quick. These look as though the trees had been stabbed by a—a dagger." She traced the fresh sticky cut as though she could heal it with her fingers.

Mr. Cooley shook his head. "He's made them to last a while."

Calder rushed on, looking at each tree she passed. She found five blazed arrows. By the base of the trees, tell-tale shavings and splinters of fresh wood littered the ground.

"I wonder what struck him?" Mr. Cooley said. "He really did a job that would certainly please your Grandmother."

"He's a traitor," Calder said. "A sneaking, under-handed traitor to the League!" She was scowling as though Walt stood before her.

Mr. Cooley pointed Louie at a circle of toadstools and neatly lopped off their tops with one slash. "Better not pass judgment until you hear what he has to say, Calder. Let's go on to the rock."

Calder stalked on silently, watching through the woods, as always, for the first glimpse of that gray shape. The light came through the trees at an angle, spreading a green haze. She turned up a little to avoid the blackberry bushes that were a landmark now and stood still. The whole right side of the rock was clearly visible. The big branch of the pine tree that used to hide the rock had been hacked half off so that it hung down, exposing the rock.

"Mr. Cooley, look what he's done!" Calder whispered.

"He must have found it was too tough for him, so he gave up."

Calder ran down through the sun-green haze of the woods to the wall that separated the wood lot from the swampy meadow. She picked up a stone from a crevice and hurled it hard at the wall. The small, dull sound was enough to set the dogs barking. Mr. Cooley watched her run across the meadow without bothering to hunt for dry places to step. Halfway across, she stopped and gave a wordless yell that floated out over the field and down the valley. The barking of the dogs rose to a frenzy. After a minute, she yelled again. Then she came slowly back up to the rock.

"I bet he doesn't dare come and face us," she said, wiping her hot face with her arm.

"You made the welkin ring, so there's no doubt that he heard you if he's there."

"He better come," she muttered.

"Calder, suppose, if he does come, that we don't say anything about the blazes until he does. It's hard for him to feel that he's going to lose the rock, you know. It looks to me as if he took his feelings out on the blazes. We'll climb up on the rock and wait a little. Here, I'll give you a foothold." Calder scrambled up on the rock and reached

153

down a hand to Mr. Cooley.

"I could wish he had put his energy into building a ladder," Mr. Cooley said as he struggled up beside her.

The dogs' barking had dropped off, and the sleepy afternoon stillness settled down on the woods. A flash of blue wings skimmed past the hanging pine bough. A darning needle lighted on the rock beside Calder, catching the sun in its gossamer wings.

"They look made of plastic, don't they?" Calder said.

"But, thank Heaven, they aren't," Mr. Cooley said.

"They might as well be. Nothing seems real up here today—those horrid blazes, nor that branch, nor—" One of the dogs yelped. "There he is!"

A couple more barks resounded across the field, but that was all. Calder stood up on the rock. "I can't see him, but I know he's coming. He has another way down around the side of the barn, so you can't see him till he gets here."

"I'm sure it's hard for him to come," Mr. Cooley said. "We don't want to seem like a high tribunal sitting up here."

Calder saw him then, coming through the woods the way he had walked on the Thruway, his shoulders slumped and his head down. How had she ever thought of her going to the cafeteria with him as a date?

"Hi," he said, standing by the rock.

"Hello, Walt, come on up and join us," Mr. Cooley said.

Calder didn't speak.

As if he was glad to be told what to do, Walt climbed up the rock and sat down as far from them as he could get.

"The League hasn't met for some time," Mr. Cooley said. "We thought we ought to get together now that Calder is released from prison, so to speak. She was incarcerated after your late adventure."

Calder looked quickly at Mr. Cooley. Why did he have to tell Walt that?

Walt was looking down at the rock. "There isn't any use having the League now."

"Why isn't there, if you still care about the rock?" Calder demanded. "Why did you have to make all those deep blazes so that everybody can walk right to it?" The question popped out before she remembered what Mr. Cooley had said about not asking him.

"So what! The whole place'll be sold. There's even been another man up here to see the rock. A man in a real swell sports car came to see Aunt Lil, an' pretty soon she told me to take him up here. He's some big shot from the city."

Calder scowled. "Why did he want to see the rock?"

"I don't know. He knew about it. He's bought a house here an' a lot of land, an' he kept saying what an unspoiled paradise it is. He couldn't get over how big the rock was. He said it oughta be where people could see it. Let 'em! There's nothing secret about it any more. The League's just a kid's game, anyhow."

"It is not! Not if Mr. Cooley is in it."

"Did you get the piece of rock for your father, Walt? Calder said you were going to take him a piece," Mr. Cooley interposed mildly.

"Yup. I took it from that piece Calder's grandmother said used to be a rocking chair. I didn't want to take

155

anything from the rock itself. I got a piece for both of you if you still want them. I hid 'em over in the beech tree.''

"Thank you; of course, we want them," Mr. Cooley said.

"Thanks," Calder muttered. "Was your aunt mad when you got back?"

"Plenty. She sent me to bed without any supper. An' I had to put my bicycle up in the barn loft. I can't get it out till she says so. I don't care."

"Did you tell her you went to see your father?"

"Yeah, but she was mad about my telling a lie about the ball team and hitchhiking. She said I'd end up in a reformatory if I kept on the way I was going." Walt looked up with a faint smile. "She was really mad."

"That's better than having her cry over you. That's what Gran did."

Mr. Cooley felt himself an outsider in this discussion.

"You're still glad you went, aren't you?" Calder asked.

Walt shrugged. "It didn't do any good; just got me in a lot of trouble."

Calder started to speak, and then didn't. The three of them sat there, closed in by the stillness of the woods.

"When did you cut the blazes, Walt?" Mr. Cooley finally asked.

"Next morning," he mumbled, not looking at them. "I got up early an' came up here. I just felt like it," he burst out. "It's still mine; I gotta right. I tried to get that branch off, but it's tough. I gotta bring a saw."

"You can see the whole side of the rock from way over there now, of course you know," Calder said.

"I know it. It still jumps out at you, though."

Calder sat twisting the end of her braid. Mr. Cooley leaned closer to examine the deep scoring of the rock. Walt stood up. "I gotta go. Aunt Lil wants to know where I am every darned minute now. She says she can't trust me." He slid down over the rock and went as far as the beech tree, coming back with two pieces of rock.

"Here." He laid them on the ground. "If you don't want them you can throw 'em away. Don't just leave 'em here for somebody to pick up easy." Abruptly, he raced off through the woods, going back by his own private way that avoided the swampy meadow.

"It's spoiled," Calder said, as she and Mr. Cooley walked back down the road, carrying their pieces of rock.

"Why is it? The rock is there."

"It just is."

"There are some things that you can't spoil, Calder. The rock is one of them."

Calder stopped to pull a blade of grass to suck. Mr. Cooley knocked a stone out of the road with Louie. They walked most of the way back to the village without talking.

14

Mr. Cooley was at dinner at the Inn, the next evening, when the waitress told him there was a boy named Walt Bolles waiting to see him. Mr. Cooley went out, carrying his untouched dessert, a piece of cream pie, and his cup of coffee with him. He found Walt standing on the porch.

"Well, Walt, come sit down. I didn't think you'd want to join me in a cup of coffee, but I thought you might be interested in a piece of pie."

"Gee, thanks," Walt murmured.

Mr. Cooley took a fork out of his pocket and handed it to him. Walt attacked the pie at once, without talking. Mr. Cooley sipped his coffee.

When he had finished, Walt began directly. "Mr.

Cooley, my aunt wanted me to come and see you because you're a geologist and know about rocks. You know the man I told you about taking to see the rock? His name's Ward. He came back again, and he wants to buy the rock before we sell the farm."

Mr. Cooley set his cup down under his rocker. "You mean the rock itself? What can he do with it?"

"He wants to move it down here to the village."

Mr. Cooley's eyebrow rose, and his mouth twisted. "That would be quite an order. The rock must weigh two to three hundred tons. How on earth does he think he could move it?"

"He told Aunt Lil he'd split it with dynamite and then cement it together again!"

"That's the wildest project I ever heard of! Where does he plan to put it?"

"He wants to set it on the common. He thinks it should be where everybody who comes to town would see it, first thing." A slow grin touched Walt's face. "It'd be right across from Calder's grandmother's house."

"It would be a good deal easier to build a good road up there so people could drive around it, if he wants people to see it and he has that much money."

"He's seen a boulder set down in the center of some town in Massachusetts, and that's what he wants to do with this one. Anyhow, Aunt Lil wants to know how much she should charge him for it. She hasn't signed the papers yet, so the rock's still ours, but she can't waste any time, and she wants to sell it before Mr. Ward changes his mind. She figures that if he finds he can't move the rock, he can still

159

own it.''

Mr. Cooley whistled. He took out his pipe and filled it. ''Well, I wouldn't know what the going price is for boulders.'' He looked at Walt. ''How do you feel about having the rock moved into town; that is supposing this tycoon could do it?''

Walt rubbed his hands down over the knees of his clean jeans. Mr. Cooley saw that he had dressed up for this call. The marks of a wet comb still showed in his hair. ''I won't be here after this summer. We're going to live in town. I don't like to think of its being down here in the middle of the village, but I'd kinda like to see what would happen when they dynamited it. Wouldn't that be something!''

''It surely would be something, something pretty crazy!'' Mr. Cooley said over the stem of his pipe.

''Calder'll be mad about having it moved,'' Walt said.

''Yes, she would be, but the rock isn't moved yet. I think there will be a good many obstacles in the way. I wonder if he has any realistic idea of the cost of such a project.''

''Oh, he's in big construction,'' Walt said. ''He'd bring his own equipment up here. He was telling Aunt Lil about the stuff he's moved.'' Walt's voice took on a tone of importance. ''Aunt Lil says it don't look like money means anything to him, the way he talks. He's here at the hotel. You can talk to him. How much should I tell Aunt Lil to charge for it?''

''I really wouldn't know, Walt.''

''Mr. Ward said he'd give her two hunderd dollars!''

Mr. Cooley puffed at his pipe. ''Perhaps she better take that offer, if she wants to sell the rock. I don't believe she'll have any other buyer," he said slowly.

"Aunt Lil says you couldn't hardly expect to get more than that just for a rock. But it isn't just any rock."

"No," Mr. Cooley agreed. "It most certainly isn't."

"Well, I'll tell her. She's waiting to hear what you think." But he hesitated a moment, swinging himself around one of the porch posts. "If you see Calder, you might tell her—you know—what's up. I sure don't want to."

The next morning, Mr. Cooley went down to tell Calder "what was up." He found her in the antique shop dusting. He went right to the point. Calder stared at him with disbelieving eyes.

"Who told that man about the rock?" she demanded.

"He saw the same postcard I picked up at the hotel desk, and he went up to look for the rock. When he couldn't find it, he went to the Bolles' farm, and Mrs. Bolles had Walt take him to see it, you remember."

"But why would he want to *move* it?"

"It seems that there was just such a boulder in a town in Massachusetts; it had been dynamited and put together again and set down in the center of town. That gave him the idea. This rock is once and a half again as big, he told me."

"Oh, Mr. Cooley, can't *anything* stay the way it is?" Calder wailed.

"Only a very few things, Calder. Even the rock changes all the time, wears, discolors—"

"That's not what I mean. I mean why can't the rock stay secret and hidden in the woods and do its weathering and

161

changing there? I suppose Walt doesn't care."

"Of course, he does, but he keeps reminding himself that he's going to town to live. And he is interested in how they'll split the rock so they can move it."

Calder gave a sharp cry of pain. "I couldn't bear to see it split. That's the worst thing I ever heard of."

The comforting thing about Mr. Cooley, Calder thought, was that he could be quiet some times, but still be with you. He just sat there in the shop, making bars of shadow with Louie across the colored squares on the barn floor. Calder sat on the antique high chair that had lost both its arms.

When Mardie came into the shop, Calder said, "Mr. Ward was the one you met at dinner that time, wasn't he? Mr. Cooley told me about his horrid idea about the rock."

"Yes, and he was the one who bought my old cherry chest; bought it right off without a word about the price; he said he felt fortunate to find such a beautiful piece. And to think he wants to buy Serpentine and put it down here on the common! He asked me that night at dinner if I would mind having it there."

"Why didn't you tell him you would?"

"Oh, I'm sure we'll get used to it, and the common really is the best place. I'm glad it will be two houses up, not right across from us."

Calder was trying to think how it would be, looking across at the rock from her window.

"I told Mr. Ward how the Development Society had been planning to make the rock more available to visitors, and I said he should talk with you about it, Mr. Cooley."

"He did this morning. I can't quite understand his

undertaking such a fantastic project in a town he has known only a few weeks. The expense will be astronomic, I should think."

"Why I understand perfectly. He's enchanted with Weldon, and he thinks the rock is so remarkable that bringing it down in the center of town will make Weldon even more special. He's already gone to the Selectmen about it. He's really offering to do a great thing for the village."

"Maybe when they put the dynamite into the rock it will break into a hundred pieces, and they won't be able to put it together again," Calder said. "Like Humpty-Dumpty!" She jumped down from her chair and began chanting, "Humpty-Dumpty sat on the hill, Humpty-Dumpty had a great spill, And all the King's horses and all the King's men couldn't put Humpty-Dumpty together again!" She went on out of the shop, and in a few minutes they saw her pedaling past on her bicycle.

"She is the strangest child," Mardie said. "I hope she isn't going to be like her father. He was always coming out with some totally meaningless quotation."

"Nothing meaningless about Humpty-Dumpty," Mr. Cooley said. "Who knows how the rock will split?"

15

Maybe this would be the last time she would ever go up to the rock, Calder thought, as she rode through the village; the last time she would have any excuse for going up the hill to see Walt, too. They couldn't very well sit on the rock when it was on the common—with Mardie right across the street and having the whole town going by. And then the dreadful enormity of moving the rock descended on her. How could the town let some total stranger walk in and buy the rock and split it up and move it! Walt's aunt would sell anything; and Walt went right along with her!

But he couldn't like the idea. He must be grieving inwardly after the way he'd tried to guard the rock. The thought of his grieving softened her feelings toward him. In

164

Idylls of the King, Sir Launcelot grieved sore. No—then Sir Launcelot was sore grieved was better. Of course, Walt wouldn't come right out and say so; he would grieve silently and be mad, the way he was when he cut those blazes.

Calder held her handle bars tight as she came to the thank-you-ma'ms and pretended she was on horseback, jumping a ditch. She dropped the bicycle on the ground at the top of the grass-grown road and started down to the sign.

The sign would look pretty silly when there wasn't any rock. Let them leave it there, like a tombstone, to remind them of what they'd lost. So much sap had oozed out along the blazes, they glistened as though they were decorated with jewels. When she got near the place to turn up toward the rock she threw a stone against the wall to start the dogs barking; it was just like knocking at the entrance to an enchanted wood. She almost liked the barking.

In the middle of the morning, the sun trickled in through the leaves and fell in wider splotches of light on the piney ground. Usually she came in the afternoons and the sun fell differently. The pine trees were dark and shiny next to the few maples and the beech tree. She climbed the wooded hill, looking at everything harder because she might not come again. The blackberries were still red and hard. She had thought she would pick them when they were ripe and sit up on the rock eating them. She stopped to run up the split-off limb of the tree the lightning had struck; there would be more broken trees after they dynamited the rock! Later, she would come up and gather the fragments of rock scattered on the ground, and take them home, and put them on her bookshelves like those broken pieces of clay or something that Dad used to have in his study. Shards of Grecian pottery, he said they were, handled by people who lived centuries ago. That was what these would be, but years and years and centuries older, and handled by the icy fingers of a glacier!

There it was, where it belonged, as sudden and startling as the very first time. How could anybody want to move something that had been dropped there thousands of years ago? "Hundreds of thousands of years," she whispered to herself, because figures didn't sink into her mind very well. Just whispering the words made her twelve years and Mother's thirty-nine and even Gran's—she wondered how old Gran was—oh yes; at the picnic Gran said she was sixty, but she looked older—made them nothing.

Calder went slowly up to the rock and laid her hands on its hard, greenish-gray surface in a silent, sorrowful greeting. She rather wished there were someone to take her picture standing here by the rock. If Walt saw her as he came through the woods, maybe he would always remember her this way after she had gone back to California. And years later they would meet—

He was awfully slow coming. The dogs had stopped barking. She climbed up on the rock. She wondered if people would try to climb up on it when the rock was down on the common. Of course, they'd have a ladder; maybe not even rustic; maybe regular steps!

Walt appeared. He had been running and was out of breath. "Hi," he said, only glancing at her. He looked sort of embarrassed. Well, he ought to.

"Hi," she murmured in a low voice, not watching him as he climbed up the rock.

"I can only stay a few minutes. Aunt Lil's got me cleaning out the barn loft. That's why I'm so dirty. I guess we'll have a sale. You oughta see all the stuff that's up there. A swell sleigh and a spinning wheel an' lots of sap buckets."

"I imagine you will have a sale. You're so crazy about selling. Even this rock." She wasn't looking at him, so she didn't see the red creep over his face.

"Mr. Cooley told you what Mr. Ward wants to do?"

"Yes, and I think it's dreadful. Some things are sacred and ought to be priceless!" Rage gathered in her mind. "How could you think of letting anyone blow up the rock, Walt Bolles? It's bad enough to take it out of its secret place in the woods, but to blow it to bits is a terrible crime. Maybe there's a spirit in the rock that will haunt you all your days. Maybe it will bring down a curse on the village that—that will spread a darkness." She ran out of ideas.

He had known she would be mad; he wasn't surprised. "Aunt Lil's selling it. Anyway, I should think you'd rather have it belong to everybody instead of somebody that doesn't care anything about it. I should think you'd be tickled about having it right across from your house."

"Well, I'm not *tickled!*" The word irritated her. Her eyes blazed at him. "Do you think I'll like looking at it and knowing it's been blown to pieces and stuck together again?"

"Mr. Ward says he has a man who knows just how to put

167

the dynamite in so it'll split clean, maybe in four pieces so they can carry 'em down the hill.''

Calder looked as if she hadn't heard him. She lay down suddenly on her stomach and stretched out her arms. "I'd like to lie right here when they come to blow it up and tell them they'll have to blow me up with it!''

"I just told you they're not going to *blow it up!* They're going to split it. It'll be something to see.''

"I think it will be horrible to see, and I'm not going to watch. Don't you feel anything about the rock?''

What did she want him to say, for gollee's sake? That he loved the rock—like a girl!

Calder turned over on her back with a great sigh. "If you lie still like this, you don't feel like yourself at all. You feel like part of the rock.''

"Say, look up at the sky and watch one cloud," Walt said. He stretched out on the rock himself. The woods were quiet; only the leaves of a poplar far over by the wall made a small sound of shivering. The sun was warm on their faces and on the rock beneath them.

"I feel as if I were moving," Calder said softly.

"Like the rock was moving." He was excited to have her feel it too. "As if it could roll right down the hill by itself and slide us off.''

"It must have rolled faster, though, underneath the glacier.''

"Yeah, I guess. Don't take your eyes off the cloud.''

Neither of them moved so much as a finger. A bird flew across the cloud they were watching. They couldn't tell whether the cloud or the rock was moving.

168

"Maybe the rock's ready to move again," Walt said. "Maybe it's been here long enough. Maybe it's always wanted to go down that road." He laughed at himself, but that was the kind of stuff she talked.

Calder sat up straight. "How could it, when it's got a whole secret hill and woods to itself? Do you think the cracks where they put the cement will show?"

"Mr. Ward said they'd look just like the scars the glacier made dragging it here."

"But it'll never be solid again, not really," Calder mourned.

Far away they could hear the thin sound of someone calling.

"That's Aunt Lil. I gotta beat it." He was down off the rock and racing headlong through the woods.

Calder followed the deep-cut blazes to the old road and went back to her bicycle. Never had she ridden more slowly down the hill. Speed seemed inappropriate for a last time. When she stopped at the Post Office, she met Barbie.

"Say, you do visit your boy friend often!" Barbie said.

"Don't be sil," Calder answered witheringly. "He comes down here, too." Well, he had once.

There were two letters from Mother, one for her and one for Mardie. They had the new address up in the corner; Calder read it over, trying to get used to it. Pacific Heights made it seem so far from here and not like home at all. She put her letter in her pocket to read when she got home.

Before she settled down to read Mother's letter, Calder stopped to look out her window down on the common. Would they put the rock where the round bed of geraniums was? Or would they take down the old bandstand that was rickety with age and much too small for the band now? But even squinting one eye, she couldn't imagine how the rock would look out there.

Without bothering to fold back the green and white quilt that Mardie was so special about, Calder got on the bed, punching the pillows up behind her, and opened Mother's letter.

Darling Calder:

I have something to tell you that may upset you just at first, but in the end, I hope it will make you as happy as I am, and you know that I haven't been happy for a long time. But unless you are, I can't be.

I am going to marry Dr. Tom, whom you have always liked. Do you remember when I first took you to him when you were about four? He cares very much about you. I think I have loved him a longer time than I let myself realize, because I was trying to make things work out with your father. Tom wants you to call him Tom instead of Dr. Tom; he doesn't want to take your father's place in any way.

Oh, Calder, he is the gentlest, most understanding person in the world, and life will be so serene with him. He has never married or had a home of his own, and he is eager to make a real home for us, which your father, with his moods and erratic departures, couldn't seem to do. I have craved this security for you. Your father knows, and he agrees that I will be happier with someone like Tom. He and Lisa are in England, as you know. When I talked with him just before they left, he seemed relieved and happy and

170

said he had had a fine letter from you.

Tom and I plan to be married next week, very quietly, but I must hear from you first, Calder. I will call you Friday night between seven and seven-thirty. I know this will be another change and a shock in a way, but I know also that you want what is best for me, as I do for you. At first, we had no thought of being married before next fall, but there seems no real reason for waiting. If you really objected, I would put it off, but I feel sure you won't do that.

And this is our lovely plan, Calder: Tom and I plan to rent a car and drive up to the Canadian Rockies, then we'll fly from there to Weldon (or as near as that's possible to do) to see Mother and bring you home with us, the middle of next month! Won't that be fun, dear, to travel as a family! I want Tom to see Weldon, where I spent so much of my childhood, and you will have to show him Serpentine Rock and all the places you have discovered. I can hardly wait to bring you back to our new home.

> *A heart full of love,*
> *Mother*

Calder had read without stopping, jumping over the words that were hard to make out in Mother's handwriting. Now she lay as still as she had on the rock, fixing her eyes on the crack in the plaster ceiling that didn't move as much as the clouds had. She couldn't believe it at first when Mother told her about the divorce. It had been so terrible when Dad really moved away, and she had waited for the weekends when he came to take her out. But she had understood about not leaving Mother alone; that she needed

171

her. She and Mother had fun together, mostly; and they did make a home. But now Mother would have Dr. Tom, and she didn't need her. Why couldn't things stay the way they were?

She liked Dr. Tom—lots. She would like his coming home every night; there was something lop-sided about a house without a father in it, but she would always feel he was Dr. Tom.

What if she did object? Mother was so sure she wouldn't do that. Why couldn't Mother have come to Vermont by herself, and they could have talked about it and gone back—just the two of them. Why did it all have to happen so fast?

"Calder! Calder, dear!" Gran stood in the doorway with both arms outstretched. "Isn't that wonderful news? Jean sounds so happy, and you will have a real home!"

Calder got hurriedly off the bed, smoothing the quilt.

"Never mind the quilt, dear." Gran sat down beside her, pulling Calder into her arms. It was good to be close to someone, to Gran, but it didn't help the feeling in the bottom of her stomach.

"Jean says Tom has been your pediatrician ever since you were a little girl, so you know him well. Why, it's the happiest thing I ever heard of! And they're coming here, Calder. In two weeks! I'm going straight down and close the shop for the rest of the day so we can make plans. I'm too excited to keep my mind on antiques!"

"May I do it for you, Mardie?" Calder wanted to get away. She ran down the stairs, jumping the last two steps, and out the door.

Under the cushion in the elderly wing chair she found her old copy of *The Wind in the Willows* that Dad used to read aloud to her. She carried it down to the hammock and let the book fall open where it would. The pages opened at the picture of Mole and Rat sitting in front of the fire in Rat's house. She began to read:

"When they got home, the Rat made a bright fire in the parlour, and planted Mole in an arm-chair in front of it, having fetched down a dressing-gown and slippers for him, and told him river stories till supper time."

She began to feel more comfortable herself.

16

The news of the man from the city who had bought the great boulder on the hill spread through the village. His name was Mr. Ward—John Ward. Overnight, everyone knew him by name. The common consensus was that he was crazy; but if he was in big construction he must know what he was doing. Also he was rich. He had bought the old Emory place and two other pieces of land. And he wanted to do something for the town. Plenty of better things he might do, but then, it was his money was going to pay for it, and at least he wasn't going to carry the rock away from here. He was just bringing it nearer.

The Selectmen of Weldon met. A town meeting was called. Half of the people in the village had forgotten what the rock looked like. Some of them had never been up to see it. Those who lived around the common weren't at all sure that they wanted that great big rock standing there, but it was shady on the common with so many trees; hard to make grass grow real well. The rock might be nice there. And, of course, no other town in Vermont would have anything quite like it. If Ward wanted to do it, at his own expense, well—let him.

It was no time at all before bright blue trucks and heavy tractors with "John Ward Construction Co.," painted on them in yellow letters were charging through Weldon, straight up the hill road that had never seen so much big equipment. A road had to be made to the rock for the heavy machinery, and the old grass-grown road that led down to the old cemetery had to be widened. You can do anything if you've got the money and you're really set on it, folks said. But Weldon wasn't used to things happening so fast or so many men and tractors put on a job at once.

Plenty of people went up now to look at the rock, and plenty of cars drove slowly past on the regular road. They couldn't even get a glimpse of the rock from the road, but they could see all the machinery: the crane and the trucks standing out there in the field and a bunk house set up for all the men on the job.

Calder wouldn't go near the hill road. She stayed around home reading, or rode her bicycle around the village, or joined Barbie and her friends. She showed no interest in the operation on the hill. She even took to looking at Gran's TV in the morning, which made Dad mad when she did it at home.

"Calder is so broody," Mardie said to Mr. Cooley, who had stopped into the shop one rainy afternoon. "She worries me."

"The idea of having the rock moved has upset her," Mr. Cooley said.

"I'd like to think it was just that," Mardie said. "She should be very happy because her mother was married ten days ago to the doctor who's taken care of Calder since she was a little girl. She's always been crazy about him, Jean tells me. It's really a wonderful thing for Calder and her mother, and you would think Calder would be as happy as a lark. But I'm afraid she's being contrary about it, although she was fine talking to her mother over the phone."

Mr. Cooley set the cradle that stood by the barn door gently rocking with his cane. "Was the news sudden?"

"Yes, I had no idea—Calder didn't either. Jean wrote both of us, oh, about two weeks ago. I'm so happy for them."

"I imagine it will take a little time for Calder to grow accustomed to the idea. She has always sounded so fond of her father."

"Her father was a terribly difficult man. He never really grew up. Clever, you know, but so erratic."

"Ah," said Mr. Cooley.

"He married again right away as soon as he and Jean were divorced."

Mr. Cooley looked out the barn door into the rain. "A divorce and two remarriages make quite an upheaval for a twelve-year-old to take, I should think."

"Children nowadays adjust very easily, if they are loved,

and Calder is certainly that," Mrs. Calder said.

"I think I'll go and look for her," Mr. Cooley said.

He found Calder on the porch on the old wicker settee, a pad of paper propped against her knees, writing. "Louie and I came to see you," he told her. "It's very dull at the Inn on a rainy day."

"It's duller here." Calder looked up at him without smiling.

"You look busy."

Calder shook her head. "I was writing a letter to Mother, but I don't feel like it." She tore the half-finished sheet from the pad, crumpled it in a ball, and stuffed it in the pocket of her jeans. "I talked with her on the telephone, anyway, and she's coming week after next. Oh, Mr. Cooley, isn't it the saddest weather up here when it rains! It's not like this at home."

"It isn't sad if you go out in it. Why don't you put on your raincoat and we'll air Louie."

"Not up to the rock! I don't want to go there," she said quickly.

"Too muddy to go up there with all they've done to the road. I thought we might just walk out the valley road. That would be easier on my old bones."

"O.K." Calder sprang up and ran to get her yellow slicker with a red rooster painted on the back and her polka-dotted rain hat.

When they came out to the road, Mr. Cooley said, "I see they took down the bandstand. So the rock will stand there. It's really coming down to live near you."

Calder's face set in silence.

177

"I thought it was a completely idiotic idea at first, but now I'm beginning to imagine how it will be. Which way do you think they'll point the over-hang?"

Calder stood still, studying the spot. "I hope they'll put the highest part toward our house, but it won't tilt, the way it does on the hill, and it won't look as though it belongs here, at all."

Mr. Cooley was slow in answering, then, as they went on up the street together, he said, "I always like to look ahead and think how things will be, but you know they usually work out better than I imagine they will."

"Have you been up to the rock?" Calder asked out of a long space of silence.

"Yes, I rode up one morning with Mr. Ward in his jeep. They have quite an operation there."

"Have they cut down the trees around it, yet?"

"They've cleared the way to the rock. Mr. Ward has such an army of men in there things are moving fast."

"I suppose Walt just loves watching it."

"He wasn't there that day," Mr. Cooley said. "But I walked up to the farm and saw him. He goes over in the evening to see what they've done. And to see the rock," he added. "Walt had that rock as his own place before you and I found it, you know. It means a lot to him."

Calder pulled off her hat and let the rain come down on her head. "I hate hats."

"Walt asked me what you had to do to be a geologist. I'm going to keep track of him. I think he might make a very good geologist."

"I might be a lady geologist."

"It's an interesting field."

"I know one thing: I'm not going to be a writer or a t-v commentator."

"They sound like rather fascinating occupations. Why, particularly?"

"I want to work with something solid and real—like rock. Maybe we should turn around now, Mr. Cooley."

"I'm afraid this hasn't been a very exciting walk," Mr. Cooley said as they reached the common.

"It isn't as interesting as going up the hill, but it isn't really the walk, I guess. It's that there isn't any excitement in me today," Calder said.

17

Since Calder had stopped going off on the hill, she had become one of a daily tennis foursome. They played each evening until it was too dark to see the ball and then stopped for a coke. Sometimes they went over to sit on Barbie's porch afterwards. Doing things with the town kids was more like being home, Calder thought, but somehow it wasn't all that much fun, and there were no unexpected adventures the way there were on the hill. The boys weren't like Walt, either; she could have real conversations with Walt.

Tonight after tennis, they all rode down to the garage to have a coke from the machine out in front.

"Boy, was that a hot game," Randy said.

"D'you want to play tomorrow morning if we can get the court?" Ted, the new boy at the Inn, asked Calder.

So he must think she wasn't bad, she thought with pleasure. "I might," Calder said. "I'll ride up around nine."

"We all might play," Barbie put in. "Oh, Calder, somebody's coming to see you!" Barbie sang softly.

Calder looked over the mouth of her coke bottle to see Walt ride by on his bike. He slowed down and then rode faster toward the common. She took pains not to hurry with her coke.

"I suppose now you won't be coming over," Barbie said. "That's Calder's boy friend," she explained to Ted.

"So long," Calder said, paying no attention to Barbie's remark. Had Walt really come down to see her? Or just to see where they were going to put the rock? There he was on the common looking at the gravel they'd spread and the machinery standing around; so that was why he'd come. She rode down the opposite side of the common and then up to Gran's, pretending not to see him until she had parked her bike.

"Oh, hi," she said, walking over to the common.

"Gosh, they've moved the bandstand already," was all he said by way of greeting. "Why haven't you been up? They got the road built—you wouldn't believe it—an' more big machinery than you ever saw—three D8 dozers, an' a compressor, an' two long low-beds, long enough to carry a house, almost. And they set up a trailer near the cemetery where some of the men cook and bunk. They had to cut down a whole pile of trees this side of the rock; it's cleaned out right up to it. Mr. Ward's paying the man who's buying the place, of course. Boy, he must be loaded. He owns all that big machinery.''

Calder listened in silence. "The dogs must bark all day long," she said finally.

Walt stooped down to pick up a piece of gravel. "Aunt Lil got rid of the dogs. Mr. Wetherall wanted Brownie."

"What happened to Fido?" Even though she had never seen them, she had a picture of each of the dogs in her mind.

"We took him to the Animal Shelter. He was getting too fierce. He bit someone. We sold the cow, too. I don't have to milk any more."

She would miss the dogs barking when she went up the hill, Calder thought. They did make the rock seem more enchanted. Then she remembered that the rock wouldn't be there.

"You oughta come up," Walt said.

"I don't want to see all that machinery and the road and the men and everything in there—not any of it."

"They're going to dynamite tomorrow. That's what I came down to tell you. It'll be something!"

"I wouldn't see it for anything; it would be too horrible."

Walt shrugged. "You might never have a chance to see such a thing again. Think what it'll be like! That big rock coming apart—like an orange falling into pieces, Mr. Ward was telling!"

The words came into her mind as suddenly as birds darting out of the sky: "I couldn't bear to see the rock riven asunder," she said solemnly.

Walt looked at her in the dusk, startled by the strange words. "You mean split?"

"Split *violently!*" Her voice vibrated with the horror of it.

"Dynamiting is sure violent, I guess. I've seen the dynamite boxes. They've got 'Hercules Dynamite' printed on 'em, so I guess it's extra powerful. The last three days, they've been boring holes. I should think you coulda heard 'em drilling way down here. The holes go down three quarters o' the way through the *whole* rock! I went over to look at 'em afterwards an' the holes make a reg'lar pattern on top so's when they load 'em with dynamite, the pressure, or whatever you call it, will be even. The man puts in dirt, too; a little dynamite and then a little dirt all the way down."

"Stop it! You can't wait to see it blown up, can you?"

Walt walked halfway around the gravel bed before he answered in a low voice. "I don't like having the rock split up any more than you do. I wisht we could keep the land with the rock on it, whaddya think? We *owned* it! But we can't, an' it's going to be split. The least I can do is to stand by. Well—you going to come?"

"I don't know."

The lights from the houses surrounding the common showed up more now; small streaks of light reached to the edge of the grassy oval and touched the trunk of a tree here and there, but left the center of the common in darkness. Walt could hardly make out Calder's face.

"You oughta come and suffer with it," he brought out at

last, not looking in her direction.

"I'll suffer just as much thinking about it," she said.

"Then you might as well be there. Mr. Cooley's going to come. He's inter'sted in seeing the color inside the rock." He waited for her to say something. When she didn't, he said, "You can watch 'em put it together again from your upstairs window almost. It's too bad you're not right across from it."

"If I take out the screen and lean out, I can see it all right. Maybe they won't be able to get the rock together again."

"Mr. Ward's got a specialist here to supervise it." Walt moved toward his bike, but once on the bicycle, he lingered. Calder hoisted herself up on the piece of old railing that was still standing.

"I got to go down to see my dad again," Walt said. "Aunt Lil drove us. Dad was glad to have the piece of Serpentine. He put it on the window sill by his bed. He says all he has to do is just look at it to be right back there."

Calder was silent, remembering the glimpse she had of Walt's father in that big room.

"The farm is really sold now," Walt said. "As soon as Aunt Lil can find a place in town, we're going to move. She don't want to stay any longer than we have to in a place that don't belong to us."

"I'm leaving here next week," Calder said. "My mother and step-father"—she brought the term out carefully—"are coming for me." Sally Wynn at home had a step-father. That was what Dr. Tom would be. In the dark, to Walt, it was possible to say it. "My mother just got married. My real father's married again, too."

"You got four parents then, sort of."

"Sort of, I guess—not really."

"You oughta come up about ten tomorrow. If you need to be there any sooner, I'll let you know." Walt wheeled off up the street.

18

Calder went over early the next morning to tell Barbie to tell Ted she couldn't pay tennis.

"I know, Randy told me; they're going to blast that big rock. Mr. Ward was telling everybody at the Inn. We're all going up to watch them. Ted's father is driving us up. Come over about eleven and you can go with us."

"I can't. I'm going to watch it with Walt."

"Say, what's so special about him?"

"He owns the rock, is all; at least his family do—or did. I'll see you there, maybe."

Walt was perfectly right, Calder thought. She should be there if everyone was going up to watch, kids that didn't have any feeling for the rock. It would help to be with Mr.

186

Cooley and Walt. Calder wore her tie-dyed jeans today with the orange shirt for strength in the ordeal; she hadn't worn them since the day they hitchhiked. Her hair was braided in two tight braids.

"If you don't let yourself think about it, this just seems like all the other times going up here, doesn't it, Mr. Cooley?" Calder said as they started up the hill road; she and Mr. Cooley and Louie.

"Not with all these cars," Mr. Cooley said, climbing up on the bank to let a truck go by.

"But when you think what we're going to witness," Calder went on, "it's like going to an execution."

"Except that the rock won't shed any blood; it will break clean and hard. I don't believe there will be any hollows in it. And then, remember, they are going to put it together again."

"Gran's always mending dishes in the antique shop, and they look awful. You can see the glue between the cracks, even though she says you'd hardly notice it."

"But the dishes didn't have cracks in them to begin with. Serpentine is scored and furrowed already by the glacier. Wait and see."

When they came to the crossroads, Calder stood still. "Oh, Mr. Cooley, just look at all that!"

Cars lined the road to the cemetery. People straggled across the rutted field, or sat on the wall. Beyond the raw new road at the upper end, bright blue trucks, and machinery, as strange in shape and gigantic in size as pre-glacial monsters, crowded together in what might have been an ancient mud wallow.

187

"You can see the rock from *here!*" Calder wailed.

The stone wall and the trees below the rock were gone, leaving the huge gray mass exposed and somehow diminished, rising out of the clutter of activity around it.

"Do not come any closer!" A man was shouting through a megaphone. "Stay *behind* the stone wall that borders the road! For fear of flying rock, you must stay back. Will people who own those cars parked by the cemetery get them out of the way. As soon as the blast is over, the road to the village must be kept clear!"

"Let's go on up to the Bolles' place and see if Walt is there," Mr. Cooley said. The man with the megaphone had started in again.

"I hate it!" Calder said. "I wish I hadn't come."

"There he is now," Mr. Calder said. Walt was coming down the road toward them.

"I was watching for you," Walt told them. He seemed so pale that Mr. Cooley looked at him closely. Beads of sweat made his hair damp across his forehead. His dark eyes moved from them up the hill and back, as though he couldn't bear to take his eyes away from the operation over there for more than a moment.

"I'll take you my secret way to the rock, and we can get above it. Nobody else'll be there. Look, we gotta go fast. Come on!"

Mr. Cooley started to say that they mustn't get too close, but held his tongue until he saw where Walt was taking them.

"This is the way I always go," Walt said.

"When you want to spy on people!" Calder made a little

face at him.

They climbed the wall into the woodlot and followed Walt single file up a series of rocky ledges. "That's my marker. Course, I don't need it, but it helps if I'm in a hurry." Walt pointed to a little pile of stones crowned with a round white cobble stone. "We can drop down now. If you keep going, you come out on a road, but it's all blackberry bushes, and you can't hardly get through."

They could hear men shouting to each other and a truck starting up, but they couldn't see anything through the trees. Walt moved swiftly, sometimes touching the tree trunks as he slipped between them. He stopped suddenly in his tracks and turned to face his followers, jerking his head.

Below them through the trees, reared the rock, but a steel ladder was propped against it, and a man stood on the top rung leaning over the rock. When he climbed down, they could see green and yellow wires coming from the top, all joined to the wire the man carried with him.

"He's going to fasten the lead wire to the blasting box," Walt explained in a hoarse whisper. "Those wires are 'tached to the sticks of dynamite. He let me climb up the ladder to see 'em do it. I was over here this morning early."

"Don't you think we're too close, Walt?" Mr. Cooley asked.

"Yeah. We'll go back up to the ridge, only I wanted you to have one last look at the rock through the trees. It's no good seeing it down below."

The three went back up to the top of the hill. Now they could catch only an occasional glimpse of bright blue and yellow machinery and the men moving down below them;

but once their eyes had found it, they could make out a gray patch of rock.

"It'll be soon now," Walt said, his voice husky with excitement.

Calder reached out and held on to Mr. Cooley's hand. Her lips pinched together in a tight line.

A man shouted something. Even up here they could feel the hush spread over the men below them and the people watching from across the field.

A dull boom resounded—not quite loud enough to fill the narrow valley or satisfy the waiting ears.

Calder let go of Mr. Cooley's hand.

"Gee," Walt said. "It wasn't any louder than a cherry bomb! The guy said it'd be loud enough to blow me to

kingdom come.''

They went cautiously back down toward the rock. The great rounded shape had separated into four craggy sections but still seemed to hold together at its base.

''Come on!'' Walt ran the rest of the way. Calder came slowly with Mr. Cooley.

One of the men glanced at them as they came through the woods, and then seeing Walt, whom they all knew by now, and Mr. Cooley, he nodded to them.

''Cracked slick as a whistle,'' he told them with satisfaction. ''Just the way we planned it; four parts about as equal as you could hope to get.''

''See, what'd I tell you! It did split like an orange,'' Walt said.

When they stood beside the split rock, they could see the inside of each piece showed deep green.

''The ridges look like little sea waves, turned to stone,'' Calder said, wonderingly.

''You're right,'' Mr. Cooley agreed. ''No cracks where moisture had trickled down and discolored it.''

Walt turned around from his close examination of the inside surface. ''I kinda hoped there'd be something—a kinda secret sign inside,'' he said, grinning sheepishly. ''Course, there couldn't be because it's solid, and nobody's ever even seen the inside before.''

''O.K. Guess you folks better get out of the way,'' one of the workmen told them. ''We're going to try to get one piece loaded before noon.''

''See how they got it dug out beneath so they can get it onto the low-bed?'' Walt pointed out. ''It isn't like an iceberg; it's just the weight of it an' all the gravel an' stuff that came with it that brought it to a stop, pitched forward, just like that—Hey! Look what's there.'' Walt pointed out the slight cleft on the outside where the tiny pink blossom of the saxifrage plant still grew.

"Ah," Calder said. "I'm going to get it."

"Took too long to wait for the flower to split the rock," Mr. Cooley said, as she came back with the shallow rooted plant in her hand.

"I want to go home," Calder said. "I don't want to watch them drag it apart."

"You don't!" Walt looked at her. "Gosh, I want to see 'em get the rock loaded. Each part'll weigh about seventy-five tons, you know. Goin' down that steep hill they wanted to use a Euc—you know, a truck to hold it back, but the road won't take all that weight, so they're goin' to 'tach a cable, somehow. A man I was talking to said he's just as soon have a stone boat an' ten team of oxen!''

"Well, Walt, you keep watch so you can tell me about it. Calder and I'll go on back home. We'll see it at the other end and watch them put Humpty-Dumpty together again."

"Mr. Cooley! Don't *ever* call the rock that. That's —that's sacrilege!"

"Aren't you the one who quoted Humpty-Dumpty to me?"

"But I wasn't calling the *rock* that! I was just talking about something that couldn't be put together again."

"Oh," Mr. Cooley said, smiling at her teasingly. "I thought at the time that was an undignified name for

193

Serpentine." But Calder ignored the teasing.

Most of the cars had started down to the village, filling the road, easing carefully over the thank-you-ma'ms, brake lights flashing on and off as they slowed for the car in front.

"Looks as if everyone but us came up here by car," Mr. Cooley grumbled, as they waited on the bank in the green, tunnelled part of the road for the cars to pass. "We might as well sit here until they all get by."

The car driven by Ted's father stopped, and Barbie leaned out to ask them to ride down. Before Mr. Cooley could answer, Calder said, "No thanks. We really want to walk."

"Wasn't that a bust!" Randy said. "There wasn't anything to see, and it didn't make any more noise than a fire-cracker!" They drove on.

"I'm sorry, Mr. Cooley," Calder said. "But I couldn't ride with them and listen to them talk about it."

"That's all right. Since we have always walked up here, I think it would be too bad to change our habit."

"The rock *was* riven asunder," she burst out. "I told Walt what it would be like."

"But if it hadn't been, you wouldn't have seen into the very heart of that great rock. That was pretty thrilling and something to remember. It was solid to the core, as Walt said.

"Yes," she said slowly. "That's a satisfaction. But I *hate* it's being split up and moved."

19

From her window Calder watched the arrival of the first piece of the rock. It lay on an enormous flat-car—low-bed, Walt had called it in that cocky, know-it-all tone of his. And it was pulled by two blue trucks that might as well be dragons, from their size and all the noise they made. The rock looked so—so naked with its green inside all exposed. The dark gray outside rounded up in a great dark hump. That was the side of the rock she had always climbed. There was the place you could dig your nails in to hang on. It was horrid to see it like this! And that Mr. Ward stood there calling out directions. She could look down on the top of his hat. She pushed up the screen so she could lean farther out the window.

The trucks—tractors, whichever they were—drove onto the green grass of the common, leaving terrible deep marks in the ground. When they came to a stop, the truck with the crane on it that had stood there for days came up alongside, but there were so many workmen around she couldn't see what they were actually doing.

The whole town, almost, watched outside the houses that faced the common. Gran and Mr. Cooley and the Canbys, a whole bunch of Gran's friends, stood just below Calder's window. She could hear them.

"When you think what all that equipment alone must cost!" Mrs. Canby's husband said.

"I hope it won't change the common; it's always made me feel so peaceful to look over there," Gran said.

"Well, I hope your Garden Club doesn't plant geraniums around it!" somebody else said.

They didn't care anything about the rock. It didn't mean anything to them, Calder thought.

Gran looked up and saw Calder. "There you are, dear!"

"You can see lots more from up here," Calder said.

"I'm sure you can, but I think it's going to be a long process. I don't believe I'll watch until they get the whole rock down," Gran said, and Mr. Canby said something about its being one of the labors of Hercules.

"Mr. Cooley, you come up," Calder said.

"I'd like to. Louie and I'll be right there." Mr. Cooley was so different from most grownups. Calder met him at the top of the stairs and took him to sit on her window-seat.

"Apparently, they've decided they don't need a superstructure, as Mr. Ward thought at first they might have to have.''

Calder wasn't listening. "Mr. Cooley, it's terrible to think how solid and . . . and tremendous the whole rock was up there where the glacier dropped it, and now it's all in pieces.''

"The rock will survive this, Calder. This is just one more tremendous ordeal it will go through; one by glacier, one by man. It's hard to measure the will of each of them and say which is the stronger."

Calder sat rubbing a mosquito bite on her knee.

"How about a cup of coffee or some orange juice and a fresh cinnamon roll?" Mardie called up the stairs.

"Thank you," Mr. Cooley called back. "We'll come down."

"Gran thinks it's a circus or a fair or something," Calder muttered, but she went.

By the time they had finished, one-quarter of the rock stood by itself on the common, and the truck with the empty low-bed had gone back for the next section. People crowded around the piece, examining it, but Calder and Mr. Cooley had no need. Instead, they stood in front of the house by the gate.

"Even a quarter of it is pretty impressive," Mr. Cooley said. "Like something from Stonehenge. It manages to make the people look small beside it."

"Why do you suppose Walt didn't come down with it?" Calder asked.

"Oh, I imagine there is plenty to watch up there on the hill."

"I'm never going up on the hill again," Calder said.

197

"There won't be much time, anyway. Mother and Dr. Tom are coming this week."

"How very fine!"

"They just got married. It's kind of upsetting, really," she added.

Mr. Cooley guided Louie carefully around the edge of the flagstones before he said, "But it won't be when you see them."

Calder lifted the latch of the gate and let it fall with a clang several times. "Mr. Cooley, you think rocks can be riven asunder and put together again, and that thinking about places is practically the same as being there—and everything's just dandy. You know it isn't true!" She was looking across at the common where the jagged edge of the section of rock reared up above the heads of the people.

"Wait and see, Calder, whether I'm telling the truth or not," Mr. Cooley said quietly.

By early afternoon the next great segment of rock arrived. Mr. Cooley had gone back to the Inn. Gran was in the house. Most of the crowd of people had left. Barbie wanted Calder to come up and watch television, but Calder couldn't bear to leave. She hung out the window watching.

"Dear," Gran called up the stairs. "Will you ride up and get some cream of tartar for me at the store?"

"Oh Gran, they're just *starting* to take the rock off!"

"They're going to be days working on that rock, Calder, so you won't miss anything."

Calder went to the top of the stairs. "Couldn't you wait just till they get the rock unloaded?"

"No, Calder. I really need it right away. You know your mother and father"—Gran's tongue sort of slithered over the "father"—"might just surprise us and come today! And I just remembered how fond of angel food cake your mother is."

"Dr. Tom isn't my father. Is cream of tartar all you want?"

Gran looked at her a moment with her sorrowful look. "Yes, thank you, Calder; that's all."

Calder went out the front door, slamming it behind her, and rode up to the store. As she came back, she watched for the first sight of the rock pieces standing together on the common, but the trucks were just pulling the low-bed out from underneath the second section. Everyone who had come to watch was quiet as the great triangular-shaped rock was slowly lowered to the ground beside the towering segment already standing there. Calder tried to bring both pieces together with her eyes; they did make her think of the broken Humpty-Dumpty in her Mother Goose book.

She went into the kitchen and put the cream of tartar on the counter where Gran was sifting flour.

"Thank you very much," Gran said. "Now, hurry back to your rock! But, Calder, you must take a bath before dinner. You look positively grimy."

The truck with the crane was moving away without bringing the two pieces any closer together. They just sood there looking like lost rocks, Calder thought. She leaned over the gate, half wanting to go back in and beg Gran's pardon, half not wanting to. She felt like being horrid. Gran had no right to call Dr. Tom her father!

Nothing more was going to happen on the common until the next piece of rock arrived, and that would take a long time, so the spectators drifted off. Mr. Ward was talking with the man who drove the crane-thing. Calder went over to look again at the hard green waves of stone. She rubbed her hand across the surface. It seemed as hard as the hardest stone in the world, but Mr. Cooley said that Serpentine wasn't as hard as granite or marble. Anyway, she liked Serpentine best.

"Well, what do you think of it?" Calder hadn't seen Mr. Ward come up beside her.

"Oh, I—" She couldn't tell him she hated what he was doing, but there was something she had wondered about, so she asked instead of answering, "Mr. Ward, why didn't you want the rock on your own land?"

He pushed his hat back on his head. "You know, I never thought of moving it to my own place. I only thought how fine it would be to have the rock down here on the common, where everyone could see it. Maybe it's the first purely unselfish construction job I ever took on! The rock was so hard to get to, where it was; nobody who came to Weldon for a day or two ever saw it. And it's really something to see. A three hundred ton rock, dropped by the glacier half a *million* years ago—that's quite a sight!"

Mr. Cooley had said two hundred and fifty thousand years ago, but it didn't matter. "I know," she said.

"And this way, I'll see it every time I drive to town. It's been quite a project," Mr. Ward went on. "There were three reporters here writing it up. Did you see them taking pictures? They'll be back when the rock's all together. One

201

of them, a smart young pup, asked me if I didn't think it ought to be called Ward's Folly when he heard how much it was going to cost me before I'm through. Maybe it should.'' But Mr. Ward was smiling at her, so she guessed he didn't mind how much it cost, really.

''But it's a surprise to me that some of the people who live around the common don't like it, I hear now.''

''My grandmother, Mrs. Calder, lives right over there, two houses down. I don't think she minds.''

''No, Mrs. Calder seemed to be quite pleased with the idea. How about you? Will you like living right beside such a big rock?''

''I—I don't really live here. I'm just visiting. Excuse me, I have to go.''

It was close to five when the heavy trucks lumbered down through the village again. Calder was in the bathtub. She had meant to be quick about her bath, but she had tried Gran's bath oil, just a few drops at first, then she held the bottle up and made green spirals with the oil until she had almost emptied it. The water was lovely and fragrant; she lay under the thick bubbles and looked up at the maple trees through the window over the bathtub. But when she heard the trucks stopping out in front, she got out of the tub without really washing, rushed down the hall letting the air dry her, and knelt on her window seat.

Walt had come this time. He was riding right beside the slice of rock, looking stuck-up proud, she thought at first. Then she saw how sober he was, and the way his arm lay on the rock, and knew differently. It was his rock, and he had had to see it dismembered in front of his eyes. Could you say "dismembered" when there weren't any limbs? Anyway, it sounded as violent and terrible as "riven asunder."

Gran wanted Calder to get dressed in her yellow linen dress, but there was no time for that. She pulled on her torn-off jeans and a shirt and sneakers and ran down the stairs, outdoors.

People had begun to collect again and were crowding around the common. Walt stood up near the rock beside the men. Even Gran came out to watch.

The truck with the crane drove slowly up until it was alongside. Calder and Mardie watched from the gate.

"My, how big it looks!" Gran said. "I'm afraid it's going to be oppressive—such a great dark mass sitting there."

"Just think, Gran, that green inside has never been seen by the eye of mortal man before," Calder said. "And never will again when the rock is joined together!"

Mardie was looking at Calder instead of the rocks. "You do dramatize everything so, Calder, just like your father. I don't think that's always a good idea. You get in the habit of making too much of everything. And I thought you were going to take a bath and get dressed?"

"I'm all clean inside, Gran. I just put these clothes on so I could go over to see the rock." She left Mardie and worked her way through the crowd until she found Walt.

"Say, you missed it," Walt said. "You shoulda seen 'em trying to get this piece loaded! It was sure a son of a gun! They had the worst time of all, an' that big chunk broke off the top!"

"Where? I didn't see it on the truck!"

"Course not. I was sitting on it coming down the hill!"

Calder gave a little moan. There it was on the ground.

"But they can fix it with this stuff they got," Walt said quickly. "It's stronger than stone even, an' it gets hard in half an hour."

"What if they can't get the pieces together tight?"

"Well, they can! There's lots of tricks to it, but the man over there with the gray hair, he knows 'em all, one of the guys was telling me."

"Clear out, you kids," Mr. Ward said. They moved back to the edge of the common, but in front of the rest of the people gathered there. Two men were taking pictures and asked them to move back a little. She didn't need any pictures, Calder thought. She could never forget how the pieces of rock looked, standing there.

"Tomorrow'll be the exciting time," Walt said. "Watching 'em pull the pieces together and cementing them. I guess they'll put the broken-off piece on last."

A woman touched Calder on the arm. "Isn't that your grandmother calling you? Aren't you Mrs. Calder's granddaughter?"

Calder looked quickly over to their house. Then she ran across the street. Mother was standing by the gate, and Dr. Tom was there. Calder buried her face against her mother.

"Calder, precious; oh, Calder, it's so good to see you! And here's Tom."

Calder swallowed down the feeling in her throat and held out her hand. "Hello, Dr. Tom."

"Hello, Calder. You arranged some real excitement for

204

us." He looked right at her, the way he did in his office, and you knew you had to let him give you a vaccination or a shot or whatever it was, but it wouldn't hurt more than you could stand.

And then Mother's arms were around her again, tight. "We just couldn't wait any longer to see you, but we didn't want Mardie to tell you for sure, for fear we couldn't get an earlier plane," Mother was saying, as they went into the house.

"She hinted when she was so anxious to have me take a bath and get dressed up, but I had to watch them take the third piece off the low-bed."

"You look beautiful to me, Calder. After all, isn't that one of your favorite costumes?"

Calder felt more natural with Mother teasing her the way she always did about her ragged shorts.

"You have a new hair cut!" Calder said.

"Yes. Do you like it?"

Calder tipped her head to one side studying it. "It's O.K." Just for a flash of a second she could see Mother on TV. That was always getting in her way. That and having kids at school ask if that was her mother, and saying how good-looking she was.

"This is the most incredible thing I ever heard of, moving that great rock down on the common! Though I suppose it will be a great tourist attraction. It ought to double the visitors to your shop, Mardie."

Mother didn't feel anything at all about the rock.

"You never wrote me about it, Calder! In fact, little one, if the truth be known, you didn't write me very many letters at all!''

Calder knew that was so. "I started two I didn't get finished," she said, and felt she had hurt Mother, saying that. She glanced over at Dr. Tom.

"You thought them, then," he said. "That's the important thing."

"Oh, Calder was so wrapped up in this rock, she didn't think of anything else. And there is a charming elderly man here this summer, a geologist, who's a great friend of Calder's. You remember, I wrote you about him. They've been off on the hills looking at rocks. Come up to your room, Jean. It's so good to have you here, and Tom!" Gran was teary and Calder squirmed.

"Let's go see if they've unloaded the rock, Calder," Dr. Tom suggested. "We took you away at a pretty bad moment to leave."

They went across to the common. "There's one more piece, of course," Calder explained. "But it'll have to wait till tomorrow now: they had such an awful time getting this last piece loaded. Tomorrow'll be the really exciting time."

20

Walt came down to the kitchen barefoot, carrying his shoes. Aunt Lil wasn't up yet, and he wanted to slide out without waking her. He spread jam on a piece of bread and poured himself a glass of milk so he wouldn't have to come back for breakfast. Maybe he'd better tell Aunt Lil. He set the glass down in the sink and tore a piece of paper from the pad on the wall.

"Have had breakfast. Going to the rock. Walt."

That would cover going down with the rock to the village, too.

He hadn't stopped to wash, but the sun on his face, as he stepped off the porch, and the air, still with a cool edge to it, made his skin feel clean. There wasn't a sound except birds.

207

He wondered if they talked to each other. Seemed like it: the way they'd call, an' then wait till they heard another bird pipe up, an' then call out again—sometimes the same way, sometimes a little different. He stood still a moment listening to them.

No one was moving around the machinery over by the wood lot. The blue trucks and the crane, sticking up as high as a tree, had been there so long now—going on five weeks—they began to look natural. The road across the field had had enough traffic on it to make it show up more than the regular road.

Walt ran all the way to the rock ledges and on up to the brow of the hill, but he slowed down as he went through the woods toward the rock. They'd cut so many trees down below that the light streamed in, flashing off a roll of heavy cable, and making a dazzle on a dozer blade on the tractor.

You didn't have to look hard to find the rock—standing in that wide cleared space—but it gave him a funny feeling to see what was left. It looked like some kind of a statue, only you couldn't figure out what it was meant to be.

This last piece of rock still belonged to him, he figured, as long as it stood there—him and his family. Once it was carried off down to the common, it wouldn't be theirs any more. In the sun the newly exposed side looked greener—real green. When the glacier dropped it, the whole rock must have been that color; the rusty streaks on the outside were due to weathering, Mr. Cooley said. This piece wouldn't be as tall as the other pieces, but it was twice as tall as he was.

Walt stepped closer, leaning against the rock so the hard

208

surface pressed against his back. The rock sloped in a little so he could lean his head back, too. He stayed that way—just still. He almost felt like part of the rock, the way Calder said she felt that time. A bird flew right across his face, as if it didn't know he was there. Against the spaces of sky, the leaves and pine needles blurred together. He felt hollow inside; maybe he hadn't had enough breakfast.

Walt knelt down on the muddy ground in front of the split side of the rock, looking for a flat enough place. There—that would do. He took out his knife and the whetstone he always carried in his pocket and honed the knife to a sharper edge. He was going to carve not just his initials—that might fit somebody else—but his whole name, Walter E. Bolles.

Maybe Serpentine wasn't one of the really hard rocks, but it was hard enough. The sound of his knife was like some animal scratching. The letters were coming out pretty even, considering, and stood out white against the green. The capital B was the hardest to make; the rock resisted the curved part. He went back over each letter to make them cut in more. He wished he had time to carve his father's name, but it was almost the same having his. Walt stood up and snapped his knife shut, dropping it back in his pocket. He could hear voices over at the trailer; the men would be coming over, and he wouldn't want to be caught doing a fool thing like carving his name. Then he took out his knife again, and down farther, way over from his, on the other side, he carved C.B. He didn't know what her middle initial was, and he didn't have time to carve her whole name. The rock wasn't hers—'cept in the way Mr. Cooley said—about

209

making something yours if you cared enough for it. She'd done that. She cared so much about it her initials oughta be on it. He didn't know whether he'd tell her or not.

He felt good about having his own name there. Nobody would ever see it because it would be sealed inside, but some day—maybe a thousand years from now, maybe after another ice age—the rock might crack open, and there his name would be. That was lots better than the initials people had carved on the outside, because it was secret. Who else in all the world had his name sealed up inside a rock, except maybe some Egyptian king, in a tomb. His was in the heart of a live rock.

One of the workmen came through the woods. "Hi! I see you're on deck to boss the last of the job!"

"Yup," Walt said, reddening a little under his tan.

Walt had to ride his bicycle down this time because there wasn't room for him on the low-bed When he got to the common, he could hardly believe his eyes. Two sections stood there as one piece, already cemented together, rounding up on top just as they used to, forming the highest half of the boulder.

Nobody could get close now. Everyone had to stay across the street from the common, but from where Walt stood he couldn't tell that the two great segments had ever been split apart. They'd done it this morning while the last piece was being loaded up on the hill. Planks lay against either side with jacks pushing them tighter. Walt looked around for Calder. He wondered what she thought now. She was over by her gate with Mr. Cooley and a lot of other folks. But she saw him, and called him to come over.

"Did you see 'em cement the pieces together?" Walt asked, the minute Calder finished introducing him to the man that was her new father.

"Of course. We watched the whole time. You wouldn't believe how fast it went. They spread on this stuff—it has a funny name. You'll see when they do other pieces. But they're going to leave them like that the rest of the day and all night, so they can't cement the other parts to them until tomorrow.

"Can you see the cement bad when you're up close?"

"You can see it all right, but Mr. Cooley's sure that when it dries it will look like all the other scars. Of course, he's always thinking everything's going to be fine."

They were silent, watching the last piece of rock lowered to the ground beside the other three sections. Walter let out his breath as though he had been holding it all during the process. "The whole rock's here now," he said.

People were drifting away now. The workmen had stopped to eat lunch. Walt lingered, feeling the knife in the pocket of his jeans.

"It must look awful up there in the woods without the rock," Calder said.

"The ground's all chewed up, and so many trees are cut down the sun gets way in there. By fall, you won't know the rock ever stood there, I s'pose, 'cept for the hole it left."

"I couldn't have stood to watch the last piece go," Calder said.

He didn't answer. "Come here. I want to show you something."

212

She went across to the common with him. Boldly, he led the way between the workmen, past Mr. Ward, right up to the piece that had just been unloaded.

"It has a funny shape, doesn't it?" Walt said.

Calder walked around the tall, pie-shaped pillar of rock.

" 'Tisn't mine any more now," Walt said.

"But it won't really belong to people down here in the village, either. They'll just look at it and go on," Calder said.

"Here—look!" Walt laid his hand on the green waves of rock.

Calder saw it then. His name stood out clearly, once you looked at it. She dropped down on her knees. "You put your name on it! Now it'll always be there, sealed in. I'm glad you didn't carve it on the outside."

Walt waited. "Do you see anything else? I didn't have time to spell it out."

She saw the initials C.B. carved on a slight depression that looked hollowed out to hold them. She traced the initials with her finger; he had carved them deep. She lifted a glowing face. "You put my initials, too!"

"I guess it means as much to you as it does to anybody," he said. "I thought you oughta have your mark on it, but I didn't know whether I'd tell you or not." He'd thought she might let out a squeal or something, the way she sometimes did, but she just sat there on the ground, going over them with her finger. When she looked up at him again, her face was sober.

"Walt Bolles, you're the most generous person I've ever known!"

He didn't know what to say. He went over to inspect the jacks.

"Calder!" Mother was standing at the gate with Mr. Cooley. "Time for lunch."

"'By," Walt said.

"You're coming down tomorrow to watch them put it all together." She didn't make it a question.

"First thing in the morning."

"Calder, would you like to invite your friend to lunch?" Mother asked, the way she always did at home. "Mr. Cooley was just telling us about him."

"No," Calder said. "He wouldn't want to come. He's suffering too much."

"Suffering?"

"From losing the rock that belonged to him and his family all these years. It was terrible for him to see the last piece brought down here to a public place."

"Oh," Mother said.

"Perhaps I can persuade him to have lunch with me at the Inn," Mr. Cooley said. "Walt!" he called. Walt was walking slowly up the street.

"Walt!" Calder called. He turned and came back. Mr. Cooley went to meet him, and the two and Louie walked up the street together.

21

Calder sat in her pajamas, writing a letter. At the top of the page, instead of the date, she wrote:

This is the day Serpentine was made whole again.

Dear Dad:

    I'm writing to tell you about the rock. Mother says you cared a lot about it when you were here. (She and Dr. Tom are married, I guess you know. I asked him, and he says I can go on calling him Dr. Tom. I'm going back with them tomorrow.)

    I told you about a man buying the rock and going to bring

it down to the common. It had to be riven asunder and dismembered (in four pieces) to do it, but now it is cemented back together again and you'd never know it unless you went up very close. The cement cracks look almost like scars the glacier made on it, and today they put on the outside pieces. It was very thrilling. The rock is the enduringest thing I know. You can't imagine how strange it is to look out and see it across the street! Mr. Cooley, my geologist friend, says it has brought the wilderness into the village. I think it must feel trapped down here and be hoping for another glacier to carry it away and smash all the houses that wall it in. But it will endure it.

When Mr. Cooley told Mother the rock is called an erratic boulder in geology books, she said that was perfect for a Vermont village because there are so many erratic people in one. And Dr. Tom said, "Aren't we all?" I liked that. Another geology book name for a glacial boulder is lost rock, because it is separated from the parent rock.

I was very depressed at first about the rock's being riven asunder and moved, and my friend, Walt Bolles, suffered greatly because it belonged to him and his family. But I feel better, and I think he does, now that the rock is put together again. It really is a mirakle. As soon as the prints that Dr. Tom took come back, I'll send you pictures of it.

Heaps and heaps of love from one erratic boulder to
another,
C.B.

She thought of telling Dad about her initials sealed in the heart of the rock so he'd understand her signing them in her letter. But she decided against it. Only she and Walt would ever know.

Before she went to bed, Calder looked out the window again at the boulder. It loomed up like a big shadow at the upper end of the common. The light from the lamppost didn't reach quite far enough to touch it. In her dark pajamas nobody would see her if she climbed up on it once more.

Calder put on her real Indian moccasins and went softly down the stairs, but a board squeaked, and Gran heard it and came out, so Calder had to tell Gran that she was thirsty.

Gran poured a glass of milk for her and stood there while she drank it. "I'm going to miss you, darling," Gran said, giving her a big hug.

Calder said good night and started up the stairs; but when Gran went back to the porch, she crept back down and slid out the back door. She bent double going past the porch where Mother and Dr. Tom and Mr. Cooley and Gran were sitting, and she didn't risk opening the gate, but climbed over the fence down by the lilac bush.

The grass of the common was muddy and chopped up. She had to be careful not to fall over any of the machinery and boards and stuff left around. The jacks were clamped against either side of the rock, holding it tight and whole. One of them made a fine thing to stand on. She slipped her moccasins off because it was easier to climb barefoot, but she scraped her knees and her stomach through her thin pajamas, squirming up to the top. Just then a car came by, catching the edge of the common in its bright lights. She lay flat against the rock until it had passed. Then she rolled over on her back.

Stars were as good to watch as clouds. The dipper hung right over her, and the Milky Way was a wispy spangled veil just floating there. The lights from the houses didn't matter; the common was a dark island under the stars.

She wished she could sleep out here all night—only it might get pretty hard. But Mother would go into her room to say goodnight. Calder stood up on the rock, her bare toes curling into the little crevices and depressions of the surface. She raised her arms up toward the stars. "I'm the King of the Mountain!" she said softly to the night and the rock. Then she slid down over the side and ran back across the street.